Destiny's Telescope

For
fara,

Destiny's Telescope

and other stories

I'll be eagerly awaiting
the tissue paper story book!

Richard Scarsbrook

Cheers!

TURNSTONE PRESS

Turnstone Press
Artspace Building
607-100 Arthur Street
Winnipeg, MB
R3B 1H3 Canada
www.TurnstonePress.com

Turnstone Press gratefully acknowledges the assistance of The Canada Council for the Arts, the Manitoba Arts Council, the Government of Canada through the Book Publishing Industry Development Program and the Government of Manitoba through the Department of Culture, Heritage and Tourism, Arts Branch, for our publishing activities.

Cover design: Doowah Design
Interior design: Sharon Caseburg
Printed and bound in Canada by Friesens for Turnstone Press.

Library and Archives Canada Cataloguing in Publication

Scarsbrook, Richard
  Destiny's telescope : and other stories / Richard Scarsbrook.

ISBN-13: 978-0-88801-315-6
ISBN-10: 0-88801-315-9

    I. Title.

PS8587.C396D48 2006   C813'.54   C2006-900333-5

For Nicole

Contents

Destiny's Telescope

PART ONE
The Principles of Motion

"Begin well and do not fear the end."
—Yugoslavian proverb

The Doppler Effect

It is six o'clock on a clear Monday morning in August. Soon the day's first diffuse planes of light will sidle lazily upward, erasing the mist from the windows they indifferently penetrate, creating tall, frail-legged shadows of tables inside Betty's Rest Stop Diner. Soon enough, the light will be bright enough to relieve the flickering neon sign of its nocturnal duties, and the diner will fill with customers.

A young woman sits outside the diner on one of the recently repainted picnic tables. The morning air is cool and dense, like a mouthful of newly liquefied ice; it swirls teasingly around her uncovered legs, sending a delightful tingle through her body. These cool summer mornings make her feel like a conductor, some small wire in an immense and complicated electronic circuit, randomly favoured to absorb a slight surge of excess current.

She breathes in deeply, as if to stop time by trapping it inside herself. She arches her back, tosses her head back, stretches herself as far as she can, in order to absorb as much of the tingle as she can. She plants her heels on the picnic table bench, her hands behind her on the tabletop, and thrusts herself towards the sky. She has become an arch, the strongest shape of all the configurations of architecture. Self-supporting. Strong. Complete.

If only she could put away some of this feeling for later in the day. This luxurious moment of cool electric prickle is like an icicle that will melt away in her hands before she can touch it to her lips.

Any moment now, another wave of cars, tractors, and pickup trucks will casually wash onto the gravel of the parking lot, and there will be more work for her to do. She sighs, and contemplates returning to the angular, fluorescent inside of the restaurant.

The plastic badge pinned to the pink collar of her waitress's uniform informs anyone interested that her name is Diane. At the moment, though, the badge broadcasts redundant information, since there is nobody inside the diner who hasn't known her name for years. A few of the Regulars sit at the counter, eating fried eggs and buttered toast, drinking coffee, wearing the uniforms of their livelihoods: loose-fitting coveralls of green or blue or brown, Kodiak work boots made dusty by the prairie wind, faces and forearms turned reddish-brown and leathery by the relentless sun, palms and fingernails blackened by machine oil, dirt, and eroded rubber from steering wheels of old tractors.

The Regulars like Diane. She pours coffee, smiles, and asks the farmers how the harvest is going. Their replies are never more than two words long, but their eyes follow magnetically behind her as she recedes from their tables. She has an unconscious talent for momentarily softening the hardened terrain of their faces: faces weathered by time, sun, wind, and too many disappointments. She reminds them of something they think they once possessed. She refills their coffee cups, and they savour the steaming liquid like a magical elixir.

The Regulars never bother to hit on Diane, though. They understand, just as much as she does, that this is all just play-acting. Betty's Diner is the adult equivalent of recess, a scheduled break from the cycles of daily life. Diane is just part of the playground. She is the imaginary princess who lives under the swing-set.

Betty, Diane's boss, is leaning forward against the yellow countertop, punching numbers into the cash register. Although Betty is past the age where most women acquire grey hair, her hair is still the colour of wheat at harvest time. Parallel wrinkles extend from the corners of her eyes and mouth, like furrows in a field. Even during years of drought or early frost, all of the farmers for miles around stop in at least once a week for breakfast at Betty's. Unlike rain, sun, and frost-free days, the food at Betty's Diner always arrives exactly as expected, on time and as ordered. Betty's Diner is like a little aside in a long tale, a sentence protected from the rest of the story by brackets.

Outside, Diane has assumed a new configuration atop the table. Her elbows are on her knees, and her chin is cupped in her hands. Her eyes peer out from beneath a lock of hair that has fallen forward, waiting. She can hear a vehicle approaching, still beyond sight. When the wind is calm, cars can be heard advancing on the Trans-Canada Highway from miles away, sometimes even before they breach the horizon.

Diane holds her breath.

Sometimes a car will slow down, the tone of its engine dropping as its speed decreases, followed then by a sustained, reverberant crunch as the tires leave the tarmac and connect with the driveway gravel. The passengers step out of the car and into the diner, for food, for a little talk, for a break from the motion. They step into the stationary existence that is Diane's life.

The headlights of this car burst free from the confinement of the eastern horizon. The sound of the engine increases in volume as it approaches, louder, more insistent, like a tribal chant, or a drum roll. The unwavering pitch tells Diane that the car is not slowing down. The car streaks past the diner, the white glare of the headlights replaced in a blink by a receding red glow, the afterthought of taillights.

The car passes, as large and loud as Diane will ever know it. It passes, and in the single moment that its approach ends and its disappearance begins, the tone of the engine drops downward.

Diane exhales slowly, refusing to let herself sigh.

The Doppler effect, she muses. *The illusion of tone shift when a sound source moves past a stationary point.*

Diane is pleased with herself, since she is surely the only person within a hundred miles of the diner who can put a name to the phenomenon.

In the dissonant harmony of internal combustion, a few of the high notes are suddenly lost, replaced by voices in the bass range. This deeper, darker tone persists for a moment, then begins to fade into silence as the taillights grow smaller, fainter. Then the red pinpoints vanish, and soon the throaty hum is swallowed by the western edge of the sky.

Diane can recall the high school science film she once viewed on the subject of the Doppler effect. The picture is jittery, and the volume on the projector turned up too high...

"The sound waves emanating from a source which is moving TOWARD a fixed point (or, the 'listener') will be COMPRESSED relative to the speed at which the source is traveling; the FREQUENCY (or 'tone') will be HIGHER. Accordingly, the sound waves emanating from a source which is moving AWAY FROM a fixed point will be STRETCHED relative to the speed at which the source is traveling; the FREQUENCY will be LOWER."

In other words, thinks Diane, *things always sound different when they're moving toward you than they do when they're moving away. Like men, for example. They always speak in sweeter tones while they're pursuing you than they do the morning after they've had you. And, just like the drivers of passing cars, they themselves never hear or feel the change.*

Perhaps this diner at the edge of the Trans-Canada Highway isn't really a diner at all, Diane muses. *Maybe it's a Doppler effect laboratory. Maybe they've put data-recording implants inside me. Maybe I'm the conduit through which the phenomenon is observed and recorded. Why else would I have been bypassed so many times?*

She slides off of the picnic table and plods back into the fluorescent glare of the restaurant, feeling much heavier than she had just moments earlier.

If I were a sound wave, she thinks, *I'd be the high-frequency kind. My moods peak and sink at least a hundred times a day.*

"Hey, Betty," she calls out. "If you were a sound wave, do you think you'd be the high-frequency kind, or the low-frequency kind?"

"Huh?" comes the expected response.

"Do you think you'd be high-pitched, or low-pitched?"

Betty drags a rag across the countertop with one hand, while arranging muffins on a tray with the other. She shrugs her sturdy shoulders. "I'm too busy trying to run a restaurant to think about silly things like that! You ought to think more about waitressin' and less about sound waves, anyway. Waitressin' is what I pay you for. Try thinking about that for awhile."

Diane gets the point, and starts to selectively wipe crumbs from the simulated-wood tabletops. She rolls her eyes, emphatically, when her back is turned to Betty. Betty is definitely the low-frequency type. Low highs, high lows. Moderate. Unwavering. On a wavelength/intensity graph, Betty would be a nearly straight line.

Diane can feel the line on her own chart plunging quickly to the bottom. One moment light with potential and inspiration, the next moment burdened with helplessness and depression.

The bell above the entrance jingles.

The door swings open with a groan, and a man steps inside. Diane can see he is wearing a brown leather jacket and jeans faded nearly white, and she can hear the syncopated clip-clop of his boot heels as he meanders towards a table.

He sits down in one of the booths. He appears to be about the same age as Diane: old enough to feel responsible for the state of the world, young enough to be disregarded by it. She takes a closer look. His hair is flattened and matted, and he is windburnt on the nose and under the eyes. Diane knows he is a motorcycle rider even before she sees the bug-speckled helmet resting on his knee.

"Great," she mutters, "just what I need. Another Motorcycle Jerk."

She continues to wipe tables. Perhaps if she keeps him waiting, makes him impatient enough, he won't bother trying to pick her up. Unfortunately, she is unable to ignore Betty's glare for long enough. She walks over to his table, looking cruelly indifferent, exercising great control over the sway of her hips. The last thing she needs is to get hit on by another passerby in clean blue jeans. She asks crisply, "What can I get you this morning, sir?"

"Hmm?" he says, tugging his gaze away from the window.

Diane rolls her eyes. It's the Nonchalant Act again. Do these men never realize how worn-out these routines are?

"What would you like for breakfast, sir?" she intones.

She says the word *sir* the way another person might say *jerk*.

"Um, bring anything, I guess. Anything but a bran muffin and grapefruit juice ... anything but that. Surprise me."

She rolls her eyes again, hoping he will notice this time. *Surprise me.* How original. She guesses that this is supposed to prove to her what an Adventurous, Carefree Type of Guy he is. Don't they ever give up?

She smiles with saccharine sweetness and asks, "What's wrong with a muffin and juice?"

He shrugs. "I've been having the same thing for breakfast every day of my adult life. I'm bored with it. I want something different."

Diane isn't sure what sort of act this one is, and for a moment she forgets to be suspicious of his motives. "What do you want then?"

He smiles wistfully, as if she has said something more than she actually meant. "I'm not sure about that yet. Just surprise me, okay?"

All of this is very puzzling to Diane. How can a man not know what he wants for breakfast? And how does he know she isn't going to bring him something simply awful?

She asks him this second question.

He smiles and says, "I trust you," and resumes his relationship with the windowpane.

Diane shrugs and walks over to the order counter, a little less methodically than when she had approached the customer's table. She glances over her shoulder en route, to check if he is watching her behind as she walks, as she is sure he will be doing. He isn't watching her, though. His gaze is still fixed on the gradually brightening prairie landscape on the other side of the window.

Diane orders a three-egg omelet, with bacon, onions, garlic, and cheese, and three slices of raisin toast with peanut butter. Betty breaks the eggs and sprinkles the other bits into a bowl, knowing that this particular combination happens to be Diane's own favourite breakfast. This causes Betty to release one of her rare, momentary smiles. *It's about time,* thinks Betty.

Diane brings a coffee pot to the stranger's table. "Cream? Sugar?"

"Both, please. Double," says the stranger.

She pours the coffee slowly, cautiously, as if the stream of coffee is a frail rope, as if she is lowering a frightened child to the safety of the ground.

"So," she says, "Where are you from?"

She does not look at him as she asks this. Better to remain aloof, detached; it's easier to bail out this way.

"Ontario," he says.

"Oh? Where in Ontario?"

He grins that strange grin again. "Name a city, and I've lived there, for at least a day or two. I never stay in one place for long. Toronto, Oshawa, Ottawa, London, Sarnia, Kingston, Hamilton, Niagara Falls, Orillia, Sudbury, Thunder Bay, Windsor, Owen Sound, Guelph, Peterborough . . . and all stops in-between. If it's in Ontario, I've been there, selling non-necessities to people who couldn't afford them."

He pauses, realizing that he has already given her a more complete answer than she likely wanted to hear. He has broken the small-talk barrier. Diane is silent, and the stranger looks down at the table. "Sorry about that," he says, "I tend to babble. . . it's a habit of my trade, which I'm trying to break. Sorry. Shrugging off the symptoms of three years in sales is proving to be more difficult than. . ."

"I was born in Ontario," Diane says abruptly, no longer feeling like being aloof. "Have you ever passed through a little town called Turpin's Bend?"

"No," he says, "sorry. Nice place?"

"There was a little river that ran through our farm, and I figured it was attached to the rest of the world. When I was a little girl, I liked to sit at the edge of the water and wait for treasures to float past. At the time, I considered things like fishermen's floats, pigeon feathers, and sun-bleached twigs to be treasures. Once there was. . ."

She blushes. "I, um, I have no idea why I'm telling you this," she stammers. "You must think I'm some kind of idiot."

The stranger smiles and shakes his head. "That's not the impression I am getting at all."

Betty hollers to Diane from the kitchen that another order is ready to be served.

The newcomer glances through the window at the highway, and asks, "Has *this* river ever brought you anything worthwhile?"

"What?"

"The highway, I mean. It's a river of a certain kind, wouldn't you say?"

"Hm," says Diane, squinting.

Betty barks out a second time, and Diane turns to hurry towards the counter. It's not a wise thing to keep Betty waiting. Then she spins again, towards the stranger.

"What's your name?" she asks.

"Barry. My name's Barry."

"I'm Diane."

She extends her hand, and Barry shakes it.

"Hi."

Diane takes a step back from the table, and her hand slides from his. "Your breakfast will be ready soon."

By the time the bloated August sun has risen fully into the sky, the restaurant is full of customers, and Diane is flitting from table to table like a housefly at a state banquet. Barry has eaten his breakfast in silence, thinking about the recent exchange between him and this waitress named Diane, trying to attach a name to the phenomenon. Was it *potential*, perhaps? It probably doesn't matter, anyway. Tomorrow he will be at least a hundred miles west of this place.

When she brought him his breakfast, she whispered in his ear.

"This has been my favourite breakfast since I was a little girl," she said.

The whisper still lingers in his ear. Needles of light reflect off the chrome of his motorcycle outside, cutting through the windowpane, igniting passing flecks of airborne dust like distant galaxies.

He pushes the now-empty plate away. He cannot remember a time that his appetite has been quite so completely satisfied. He could sit here in this booth all morning, basking in the dusty sunlight, but he cannot quite forget that he still has a lot of ground to cover. The Rocky Mountains aren't going to get any closer by him sitting in a diner in the middle of the prairies.

A sigh of resignation, a deposit of money on the table, and Barry rises with his helmet tucked under his arm.

His motion is detected by Diane's peripheral vision, as she randomly dumps a load of coffee into another empty vessel. There goes another one. Lately, she can hear the Doppler effect before it even occurs.

He pauses at the door. She is at the other end of the restaurant, which, at the moment, seems more like a tunnel than a room.

She sees him standing there, backlit, like a spirit.

He waits, feeling her quick glances like pinpricks.

She continues with the coffee.

He waits, watching her trying to ignore him.

She starts to take another order.

He sighs, and pushes the door open.

"Could you hang on a moment?" she says to the customer. She is already halfway to the door.

He is swinging a leg over the seat of the motorcycle when she catches up with him. He hasn't put his helmet on yet.

It is one of those moments in which something twists, a moment in which something is obscured at the same moment it is revealed. It is something between exhilaration and fright, and neither Barry nor Diane is sure what to say to the other. This is something that can be perceived but not explained, something that eludes the specificity of words.

They stare at each other, surprised by the forces that draw them together.

"When are you finished work?" Barry manages.

"Six tonight."

"I'll pick you up."

"No. I don't like motorcycles. They scare me."

Barry doesn't even pause for breath. "We'll walk, then."

Much to her own surprise, Diane nods yes. Then she vanishes into the restaurant, unable to exhale.

Barry starts the motorcycle's engine, turns back the throttle as he lets out the clutch lever. A roar of power from just outside himself; the vibration of the handlebars almost cancels out the shaking of his hands.

They have carried the picnic table behind the restaurant, and are sitting together on top of it. They are leaning against one another, watching the sky turn a solemn shade of red. They are wedged like molecules between an expanse of land almost as endless as the bowl of sky above it. The surrounding oceans of wheat ripple and swell with the evening breeze, like tanned skin over flexing muscles.

Question Period begins.

"Why don't you like motorcycles, Diane? Have you had a bad experience or something?"

"Nope. I've never even been on one. They're dangerous. Too fast. Nothing to protect you."

"It depends on how you ride them. If you're careful, and if you don't take stupid risks, you're okay."

"Oh, come off it, Barry!" Diane laughs. "Your motorcycle has the biggest engine I've ever seen!"

Barry shrugs. "It's a CBX. It's got a six-cylinder engine. Even the biggest bikes normally only have four. It's got the largest engine ever put onto a production motorcycle. They don't even build them anymore. Too many smart alecks getting themselves killed, I suppose."

"So why did you buy it? Suicidal tendencies? Delusions of immortality?" She grins. It seems like whole eras have passed since she was last able to comfortably poke fun at a man like this.

But Barry remains serious. "It represents a shift in my purposes."

"Hmm?"

"I'm not sure if I can explain this, but I'll try."

He clears his throat. "I've been spending my life inside boxes of one type or another ... subway cars and buses and airplanes, apartments, offices, beige-walled hotel rooms. I was watching television one night, and there was this commercial for motor-cycles ... this guy was riding through the centre of this incredi-ble prairie landscape, and all around him was sky and ground, passing like history. This got me really thinking—a TV commer-cial, if you can believe it—about how amazing it would be to just move though sky and land, with no buildings, no windows to box in your view of the world."

Diane gestures towards the motorcycle.

"So where does the Supertoy fit in to all of this?"

"No windows. No walls. Just excess," says Barry. "It has more power than I'll ever be able to use. I just enjoy the feeling of knowing it's there."

"Excess?"

Barry's eyes bulge out, as if he has an idea too large for his brain to hold on to. "Yes! Excess!" He chirps, "No restrictions! No limits! Excessive speed! Excessive scenery! The road moves underneath me and the scenery moves past and the clouds twist and transform overhead, and it's all mine. It's like swimming underwater with your eyes open, except it's faster, you can see further, and there's no danger of drowning."

Diane sighs. She can feel herself sliding over the top of another sound wave, slipping downward, as if through deep, cold water. He is wrong about something: It is possible to drown on dry land.

"I suppose it's a nice place to visit, Barry."

"You mean you don't like it here? I can't imagine it!"

His voice falls as he says this. Was that the Doppler shift she just heard in his voice? Is he already moving away?

Diane tries to explain, tries to keep her head above the surface. "All of this excess can get to you after awhile, that's all. When there aren't any borders around you, it becomes difficult to focus on anything. So you turn your focus inside yourself, where it's smaller, where you can pick out the details. And you start finding things that maybe you didn't want to find."

"Like what?"

"Like the past, I guess. Things look a lot different to a resident than they do to a passerby."

They withdraw into their own private thoughts for a while, wanting desperately to understand each other. Diane can hear a car approaching from the east. It passes, unaware that it has even been heard. The only possible intrusion into its single-minded motion is the flickering light of the neon sign.

There is a long, dense expanse of silence before either of them speaks again.

"Have you ever heard of the Doppler effect, Barry?" she asks, already convinced that he hasn't.

"Hmm?" says Barry, as the unexpected words penetrate the invisible barrier of silence. He leans forward, emerging into the open again. "I've heard of it," he says. "It has to do with the light radiated by moving stars, doesn't it?"

"Stars?" she says, "I thought it had to do with sound. Explain it to me."

"Well," he says, "the light cast by stars can be broken into a spectrum, right? One side of the spectrum is blue, and the other side is red, like in a rainbow. If a star is moving away from you, its spectrum shifts to the red side, and if it's approaching you, it shifts to the blue. Either way, it's the Doppler effect."

Both are looking skyward. It's like a big, upside-down black bowl, decorated with shimmering flecks of light, but both know that it is much more complicated than that.

"They say that most of the stars in the universe are red-shifting," whispers Barry, "which means that the universe is getting bigger."

He pries his gaze from the sky and looks at her. What a beautiful woman she is. She makes him think that perhaps there actually is a God nestled somewhere up there, beyond all of that floating matter and black void.

Diane continues to look up, but she can feel Barry's eyes upon her now. It is a comfortable feeling, as natural as the light of the moon on the back of her neck. Possibly, she thinks, Barry is the difference between sound and light. Perhaps he is not a sound wave like the other men, but the traveling light of a star, a message from a single point in an expanding universe.

"Some stars are blue shifting, you know," says Barry. "Some stars are moving towards each other, even as the matter in the universe continues to spread apart."

Like stellar motion, her arms place themselves around his neck. They kiss, and for a moment, sky and earth and stars disappear, irrelevant.

"Why did you ask me about that anyway? Kind of an odd question, don't you think?"

"I'm seeing blue," is all she says.

The whole sky has moved before their lips part again.

"I'm not afraid of motorcycles any more," she whispers.

And the universe, as far as science can tell, continues to expand.

The Twilight Girl

(Sunday)

Twilight. That little space in time each day where the colourful, sunlit world of normal people overlaps with my own grey existence. Twilight is when I meet with Rachel.

Usually, Rachel and I play games or sing songs or tell jokes, and Rachel tells me about the daily exploits of the other children who attend her school, and I laugh and wonder at it all. Rachel's tales of the daytime world fascinate and delight me, give me a glimpse into their world of colour and brightness. When I look at Rachel's long, thick, black hair and her bronze skin, and then I look at my own translucent, waxy white shell, and I feel the wispy fibres atop my head, it is as if Rachel and I are beings from two different planets. Still, Rachel's stories make me feel, for a little while, like a light, crisp leaf released and carried from the shadow of the tree by a friendly current of air.

This evening, though, was different. This evening I felt more like a small, grey stone, sitting at the bottom of a deep, cold lake. This morning, something happened which reminded me that the glimpses Rachel brings me of her sunlit world are ones I can never completely share.

My name is Luna, after the moon which dully illuminates my life. For twelve years now, since I was born, I have had a condition called *porphyria*, which means that I am allergic to sunlight. My parents, who both have a much milder form of porphyria, first met at a university laboratory in Toronto during a medical study of the condition. My father came from Prince Rupert, BC, which receives the least amount of sunlight of any place in Canada, and my mother came all the way from South Africa, where she lived in a windowless house, painted white on the outside to reflect the sun's rays. I can understand Mom's desire to stay in Toronto, but Dad's? Anyway, in Toronto my parents met, fell in love, married, and, stupidly ignoring the reality of genetics, decided to have children. Dad's porphyria-carrying seeds and Mom's porphyria-carrying eggs first combined to make my brother Adam, and, four years later, me.

Rachel thinks the word "porphyria" sounds like the name of a pretty tropical flower. I told her that I think it sounds like the name of a red-skinned, fire-cloaked demon, whose very presence melts people's limbs like candlesticks in a furnace. She shrugged her shoulders and said she was only trying to be positive.

It's difficult to see anything positive about our condition when you see the effect it has had on my older brother. Mom and Dad found out about Adam's condition the hard way. They were having a picnic lunch on a cool, overcast spring day, one of the few days all year it seemed safe for them to go out. They sat under a huge maple tree, just in case the clouds broke up and the sun came out. Mom and Dad thought they had taken every precaution to protect themselves. For some reason, they assumed Adam had escaped the curse of porphyria, because he had never shown any signs of having it. He hadn't shown any signs of having it because his parents never went out into the sunlight.

Adam was just old enough to crawl, and, lured by a glimmering piece of crumpled aluminum foil, his little hands and knees carried him out from under the tree's foliage just as the sunlight broke through the clouds. By the time Dad sprinted over to grab him, Adam was shrieking as if his lungs were full of molten metal, and that's probably what it felt like. Blisters and lesions were already breaking out on his tender baby skin. His throat swelled up so he could hardly breathe. He threw up. He had diarrhea. The wispy strands of hair on his head fell out within a few days. It was a difficult way for Mom and Dad to discover that Adam had a more severe form of porphyria than either of them did, but I imagine it was much worse for Adam.

And maybe it happened as early as that. Maybe that day he was all burned up as a little baby was the day that Adam became the way he would be for the rest of his life, boiling over with rage and anxiety.

Mom, Dad, and I would try to sleep during the sunlight hours, with the air conditioners buzzing and the special fluorescent lights turned off, but Adam would often pace around our dark house for hours. Sometimes, he would tiptoe out into the living room and open a crack in the door and peek out at the daytime children playing in the park across the street, and even as that slender beam of sunlight cut a sizzling vertical wound across his face, neck, and wrist, he would watch and listen. He would hear the happy squeals of the daytime children, and a sound somewhere between sobbing and howling burst out from deep inside his lungs. Then, one day, when there was no sobbing left inside him, Adam ran howling out into the sunlight.

The first time he ran out of the house like that, he was in the hospital for a week. They had to smother his blistered skin in ointment, and wrap him from head to toe in bandages. His teeth softened and rotted, and many of them fell out. His hair grew back only in patches, like pictures I have seen of farmers' crops during a drought.

The second time Adam ran into the sun's searing light, he ran nearly half a kilometre from home before finally collapsing. The doctors said some of his exposed skin was like overcooked bacon. They had to float him in a tank filled with special fluid. He didn't come home for nearly three months. They had to seal off all the windows in his hospital room with reflective foil and tape, and they installed a special air conditioner to keep the rest of his skin from falling off. They gave him drugs to make him sleep, so he wouldn't howl so much, but I'll bet he just howled in his dreams instead.

Then, yesterday afternoon, when the sun had just passed its highest point in the sky, Adam ran from the house for the third time, wearing only a pair of shorts. The police found him this morning, huddled in the shade of a sewer-pipe opening, wrapped in his own arms and legs like a baby inside its mother. An ambulance rushed him to the hospital, but he was already dead.

Mom and Dad haven't said a single word, to me or to each other, since they got home from identifying Adam's body. I guess he must have looked pretty bad.

Adam used to joke, without laughing, that it would be funny if he died on a Sunday.

"*Sun* day," he would taunt, "get it, Loonie?"

"Ha ha, very funny," I would respond. "And quit calling me 'Loonie'!"

Thank goodness Adam was the only boy I ever saw on a regular basis. If I went to school with the daylight kids like Rachel does, I'd probably have dozens of boys calling me "Loonie" all the time, and I'd probably hate my parents for giving me such a name.

I guess I shouldn't complain. There won't be anybody to call me "Loonie," now.

Rachel touches me on the shoulder, and I jump.

"You okay, Luna?"

"I guess."

"I'll come around to see you tomorrow, okay?"

"If you want to."

(Monday)

Rachel shows up early at my house this afternoon. Usually, she comes after her dinner time, but today she's here right after her classes end. It's been dark and rainy all day, but I didn't know it until Rachel showed up with her wet clothes clinging to her body and her hair hanging in ringlets. You don't notice much about the weather outside when you live in a house with blacked-out windows.

"It's Monday," Rachel says, "the day named after the moon. You're also named after the moon, Luna, so it's your day, too."

"Whatever," I say. Rachel would have me believe that everyone in the daylight world is this optimistic, but we have TV, so I know that most of them aren't.

"There's no sun today at all," Rachel tells me. "It's even darker and cooler than when we usually meet—the rain is supposed to last into the night."

She takes me by the hand. "Have you got a raincoat?"

"Why?"

"I want to show you something. Come on."

"Whatever," I say.

As I approach the door, you would expect my parents to try to stop me, especially after what happened to Adam yesterday. But they just sit on either end of the couch gazing into different regions of nowhere. Nothing can penetrate their grief.

I suppose Rachel thinks that this little walk will cheer me up, make me forget that there is only the thinnest layer of cloud outside between me and the sun that killed my brother yesterday. I plod along behind Rachel. We walk for a long time, saying nothing. After a while, we are stepping through wet grass, clingy wet weeds, and the water in the spongy ground squirts into our sneakers. Then there is sand beneath our feet, which forms a crust around our wet shoes.

"Look up, Luna," Rachel says.

The whole time we were walking I watched the ground passing under my feet, but now I look up. Ahead, open water stretches out to the horizon. I have never seen a real lake before—they tend to disappear in the dark. It's so beautiful! I am unable to exhale.

"This place is called The Beaches," Rachel says.

I gaze out over the water. It's much bigger than I thought. I've only seen Lake Ontario on TV, and in a picture in an atlas which was taken from the top of the CN Tower, which I've also only ever seen at night. But now I am seeing the lake for real, with my own eyes. There is enough light for me to see, yet enough darkness for me to live.

Tears are running down my cheeks. I am crying. I never cry.

"This is . . . so . . ."

I don't know what to say. It's too much.

Then, a fear jolts through me. I'm shivering, covered in goosebumps.

"Sunlight!" I yelp. "I've got to get inside!"

"Relax," Rachel says. "It's just a sunbeam. A ray of light breaking through a crack in the clouds. It's miles away, Luna."

"What if the clouds crack open right above me? They'll be burying me with my brother tomorrow!"

"Not very likely. But we can stand under that tree over there if it'll make you feel any better."

"It would."

I must admit, from beneath this tree that sunbeam is pretty. And bigger than on TV or in pictures. Everything out here seems enormous. And more scary. But also more real.

And now something absolutely amazing is happening in the distance, almost at the line where the water meets the murky sky. It's . . . overwhelming! The colour! The beauty of it! It covers half the sky. It's a hundred times more incredible than the starriest night-time sky.

I have never heard such sounds coming from inside of me. I have never cried before, and now I can't seem to stop.

"It's a rainbow," Rachel says. "Nice, eh?"

"Oh. Oh yeah." I am barely able to sneak the words in between the little staccato gasps which shake my body. "Oh. Oh yeah. Oh."

(Tuesday)

Last night I forgot to ask Rachel what Tuesday is named after. I also forgot to ask her if she believes in heaven. I'm still not sure if there is such a place, but I think Rachel would know.

Tonight, under the dim light of a crescent moon, we will bury my brother Adam, and I still can't decide if there is a heaven or not. As a little girl, I believed in it, but lately I've been finding the whole idea a little hokey. Now I want to believe in heaven again, with the unquestioning faith I had when I was small. Now this seems like a very important thing. I want to believe that there is more in store for Adam than just an eternity buried in the ground, isolated forever in the cold and the darkness he struggled to escape for his whole life. I want to believe there are sunbeams in heaven, and I want to believe there are rainbows, so Adam can see that it isn't all bad, that the light isn't always the enemy.

I want to believe in a heaven like that.

Symbols

At the top of the Peace Tower, a Canadian flag crackles and snaps, defying the harsh November wind. It is one of the larger flags of its kind, yet against the murky sky it seems small, almost fragile.

It is past dusk, and the grind and clatter of the city has receded to a slumbering purr. It is this night-time wheeze which has called Theodore Blinker out into such an unwelcoming night. Theodore is a country boy, and country boys are made restless by the night sounds that city folk mistake for silence.

Theodore is known to everyone but himself as Teddy. He wears loose-cut work jeans, canvas sneakers, and the tattered plaid jacket that has been part of his uniform since the awkward days of adolescence. A teenage girl on the bus once asked him where he bought the Scarborough tuxedo. Theodore didn't get it.

The words of Theodore's brother Michael roll over and over in his mind. "Go to Ottawa, kid!" Michael had said. "For God's sake, don't just mope around the farm! There was nothing you could do about it! Feeling sorry about it isn't going to change anything! Get out there and start living again!"

Those were Michael's words to Theodore as they peeled away their black suits and loosened their ties in front of the warped mirror they had shared as boys. Theodore listened, as always. He looked at Mike's snowblade chin and laser-green eyes. Then he looked at himself, with his untameable cowlick and his cartoon-puppy-dog eyes, and he wondered to himself how the genetic roulette wheel could have been so kind to his older brother while being so utterly merciless to himself.

"No sir, there's not another city like it in Canada," Michael repeated. "Go there, Teddy! Go to Ottawa! Go find yourself in the city! Look at the symbols! The truth waits for you in the city!"

So as to seem not ungrateful for the advice, Theodore packed a small suitcase, withdrew some money from his account at the Farmers' Credit Union, and caught the early train to Ottawa.

Nearly two months have passed now, and, contrary to Michael's guarantees, Theodore has not *found himself* yet. He is dry as parchment, and perhaps as brittle. He feels as if he might crumble to dust at any moment.

His feet seem to know where they are taking him. These are the same streets that his brother Michael had purposefully trodden every day during his brief stay at the university. If Theodore's own shuffling walk has any purpose, he certainly doesn't know what it is.

"Make sure you take some time to have a good look at the Parliament Buildings, kid," Michael had said. "You've heard about the time that Parliament burned down, right? The Library was all that was left standing. A symbol of the durability of knowledge, don't ya think?"

Theodore had simply nodded yes. He never had much choice but to agree with such statements from Michael. After all, Michael had been to university, and, to Theodore's way of

thinking, that fact somehow qualified Michael to know everything that Theodore himself had not picked up during his five
years of struggle at high school.

"And the Peace Tower ... the tallest peak on the whole damn
thing ... just the name symbolizes Canada's role in the affairs of
the world, eh? Eh? It'll put things in perspective for you. It'll
show you where you really stand in the grand scheme of things,
Teddy."

Under different circumstances, Theodore probably would have
thought about the symbolism of the Peace Tower and the
Library of Parliament as he approached and passed them. He
probably would have even looked up at the fluttering Canadian
flag, his heart palpitating with patriotic emotion. He probably
would have even taken a picture.

Circumstances being as they are, however, Theodore stumbles blindly forward, face-first into the wind, past these glorious symbols. Fortunately, a tall, black, wrought-iron fence pre-
vents him from wandering accidentally over the edge of the cliff
above the Ottawa River. He stops, startled by the sudden intrusion of the fence into his foggy consciousness.

He climbs over the fence, onto a slim ledge of rock, and peers
over the cliff's edge into the Ottawa River. The wind batters the
foam on the water's surface. As he used to do with clouds,
Theodore looks for images of things in the foam, but everything
twists and changes too quickly to pick anything out.

His vision drifts slowly along the river and off to the right
through the Rideau Canal, then up the steep slope to the
National Art Gallery. Michael hadn't said much about the
gallery's contents, but he had certainly been impressed with the
way the building looked at night.

"It has this huge geometric glass dome, see," he had
explained, "and it's very moving to see it at night—very symbolic! The darkness of the night is like spiritual disillusion, but

the art gallery shines bright, symbolizing the spirit of human creativity! You'll agree with me when you see it, 'cause you're an observant kid, Teddy!"

But, as he stands behind the Parliament Buildings, with his back against the fence at the edge of the cliff, everything spread before him like a patchwork picnic-blanket of symbolism, Theodore Blinker does not notice anything more than random patterns of foam skittering haplessly across the dark surface of the water.

How could he notice anything outside himself when most of him had been taken along with Sarah?

In his mind, Theodore can see her now, more vividly than a photograph. There were things about Sarah that no camera could ever capture, qualities that could never survive such captivity. Trying to freeze a moment of Sarah was like trying to capture the wind in a jar. Yet, in his mind, Theodore can see her in the same way one sees the roar of a waterfall.

She had the most beautiful hair he had ever seen, long and shiny, with all the shades of gold of an autumn field of sun-bleached corn. When she tied it in braids, it was art, and when she let it cascade down over her shoulders, it was nature. He was going to give her the poem he had written about her hair, but, of course, he couldn't do that. Michael, who had learned about such things at university, told him that to write about any individual part of a woman was to objectify her, which made her less than human. Theodore would have never dreamed of insulting Sarah in such a way! He thought he was doing something *nice*!

So Theodore did not give her the poem he had written about her hair, nor the poem that described the warm, clean, baby-powder touch of her fingers against the small of his back, nor did he give her the one he wrote about her eyes—her wonderful eyes, orbs of earthy green, the colour of life as seen from space.

He didn't give Sarah the promise ring he had bought for her, either. Michael had barked like a drill sergeant when he saw it. "Come on, Teddy! The nineteen-fifties are over, for Chrissakes! You can't just stake claim on a woman like that! You're insulting her individuality if you do, and ..."

"She can give it back later if she changes her mind," Theodore had said quietly.

"Teddy, Teddy, Teddy," Michael had moaned, throwing an arm around his brother's shoulder, "Don't be such a slave to the past! *Evolve*, for cryin' out loud!"

After much consternation, Theodore finally gave in to Michael's better judgement and returned the ring to the jewelry store.

Less than a week later, Sarah was dead.

Her family decided that a closed-casket ceremony would be easier on everyone involved, since she had been messed up pretty badly in the accident. It was unfortunate that nobody thought to tell Theodore, for it would have spared him the inconvenience of carrying that little wooden box around the funeral parlour all day.

"It's so sad to see one go so young," people would confide to Theodore as they shook his hand and passed along. Some of them would ask, "Hey, kid, what's in the box?"

Theodore had spent dozens of sleepless hours constructing the little box, which was no larger than a hardcover novel. It was made from dark, knotty oak, which he had cut from the fallen tree where they used to sit and hold hands and kiss. Sarah would point out to Theodore different constellations of stars, and sometimes Theodore would identify the calls of night creatures.

Inside the little box, Theodore had put all the poems he had ever written. There were about twenty of them, and they were all about Sarah. He had meant to slip the box into her casket so something from him could be with her forever. He didn't tell anyone, not even Michael. Michael probably wouldn't have seen the point.

Theodore had slowly edged his way towards the casket, putting on a face of granite, and bracing himself for the blow of seeing Sarah without that familiar flush of life upon her cheeks.

The casket lid was already shut when he arrived. Nobody had told him it would be closed. Theodore walked back to the greeting line with the box clasped in his fingers.

During the service, many comments were made about how well Sarah's boyfriend was taking the whole thing. Theodore would not give in to such indulgences as crying. Sarah had been able to tug the spirit from his slouchy farmboy body and send it soaring skyward, simply by touching her long, slender fingers to his face, and now she was gone. But he would bear it. He would bear it.

After most of the mourners had trickled away from the gravesite, Theodore remained. He knelt on the cold grass, stretched his arm deep down into the rectangular hole in the earth, and gently laid the little box atop the arched casket lid. It immediately slid off.

He watched with horror as it tumbled into the dark crack between the casket and the wall of earth beside it. The darkness of the crevice absorbed the box completely. Theodore remained there, kneeling and staring, and he would have stayed there all night, if his brother Michael had not come to fetch him home. As they walked towards the car, Theodore told him about the box. Michael squinted and stroked his chin, the way he often did when he meant to show that he was seriously contemplating something.

"Maybe the box is a symbol, Teddy. Maybe it represents a part of you that's fallen away, that can't be retrieved."

Michael grinned to himself. *What would they do without me? Who else could decipher such a moment?*

"Best just to let go, Teddy," Michael brayed. "The box is gone, and so is your connection to Sarah. Just let it go."

If it had just been a piece of me falling into the darkness, Theodore now thinks, it would be a much simpler matter. I would feel much lighter. It would be less difficult to carry on.

But, whatever of him had fallen into that hole in the earth, it had displaced an equal portion of the hole's darkness, and the darkness had somehow crawled inside him.

Theodore spreads his arms wide, thrusts his chest towards the river, which swirls and foams beneath him. *For a moment, I will soar. Then, the cold, the darkness will grip me, pull me under. I will not fight back. I will welcome the water into my lungs, absorb its searing cold. I will not gasp or struggle; I will give what's left of myself to the cold, to the dark. And the pain will end.*

He closes his eyes and bends his knees, to spring out into the wind. But there is a sudden loud chattering noise at his feet. It comes from the wall of bushes around the iron fence. Theodore glances around, wide eyed. The chattering becomes louder, and Theodore recognizes the noise. Sure enough, a fuzzy baby raccoon stumbles out from the bushes onto the ledge, at his feet.

"Here," whispers Theodore. "Let's put you on the other side of the fence, where you won't fall."

He reaches for the little animal, when another very large raccoon crashes through the bushes. Its fur is standing on end, its back is arched high, it snarls and hisses.

"Shit!" yelps Theodore, as his feet slip from the ledge.

He grasps wildly at the fence as his feet give way beneath him, and manages to grip one of the thin iron posts with his right hand. He pulls himself back from the brink, scrambles to his feet, and jumps back over the fence before he is even fully aware of what has happened.

He spins around, towards the fence and the hedges just beyond. The raccoons have disappeared.

Theodore is finally able to blink. He sits down on the cold ground cross-legged, shivering and laughing. Yes, laughing, for the first time since the accident. He laughs and laughs, rolling around on the grass, kicking his feet at the sky.

If only Sarah could have seen this! Nearly killed by a raccoon!

She would have laughed at him, in a happy, taunting way. They would have laughed together. She would have cooed softly in his left ear, telling him what a Brave Knight he was, and the skin on the back of his neck would have tingled pleasantly.

And, without noticing the transition, Theodore is crying. He lies on his back on the cold, crisp grass, sobbing, his lungs clawing for air, hot tears streaming down his face, filling his ears.

"Sarah!" he cries. "If only you knew how much . . . if only I had told you how much . . ."

He lets out a howl of sorrow, which vanishes immediately in the indifferent wind. Then, a cry of anger, and one of frustration. They too are devoured by the snarling gale.

Then, for the first time since he left the apartment, Theodore hears the flag crackling high above him. He looks up, far up at the top of the Peace Tower. There is the flag, flying nearly straight, fighting, snapping, refusing to give in. Despite the power of the indifferent wind, despite its overbearing roar, the crackling sound of the comparatively tiny flag can still be heard. As soon as ears hear it through the roar, as soon as eyes see it through the darkness, its presence cannot be forgotten.

Theodore rises, stands motionless, watching, listening.

I wonder if this is a symbol. I'll ask Michael when I get home.

The next morning, he gets on a bus that takes him back to the farm where he grew up.

Theodore Blinker has decided to survive.

Traffic Jam

The sound of a car crash is not easily forgotten.

It's like the sound of the nearby clap of thunder, which rattles your apartment window and makes you jump from under the covers, your heart bursting with sudden adrenaline. It's like the unexpected crack of the rifle, which snaps the silence of a walk in the autumn woods, makes you think for a split second that you feel the bullet in your chest. It's a sound that is loud and quick and definite.

It's the sound that the midnight blue BMW coupe made as it smashed into the rear end of an orange cement truck.

It could have just as easily been a black Mustang, with yours truly behind the wheel. I had been cruising southwest along the Don Valley Parkway, heading downtown to work on a Monday morning. The sun was blazing through the driver's side window, bringing the world through the glass in vivid 3-D Technicolor. For the first time in many months, I looked beyond the concrete banks of the freeway, and noticed the lush greenery of the valley coursing past the Mustang's tinted windows. As I eased the car though the last long curve in the parkway before the exit to downtown, I felt a little bit of the delight I used to feel when I started making this daily drive a few years ago.

It's only been three years, but somehow I felt much younger then. Sometimes at night, when I was working late, I would stop and sit with my chair turned away from my desk and gaze out my reflection on the window of my little office on the twenty-first floor and try to pull the nighttime glow of the city into myself through my eyes. I would leave the office and wander along the streets of downtown, gazing up at the towers that stretched up into the sky, drawing deep breaths as if to draw all of that tall, bold architecture into my lungs, to make it part of my being. I hummed along to the chorus of screeching streetcar wheels, the plaintive echoed wailing of firetruck sirens six blocks away, the roar of subway trains that rushed up through the grates in the sidewalk. The sounds of the city swirled around me, refreshed me and opened my mind.

Compared to the quiet, wide-open space in which I had spent my life until then, everything about Toronto was vital and thrilling and new. It was almost like falling in love for the first time.

Lately, though, it no longer feels like I'm moving at all. I feel as if I am a fixed point, and it is the city which surrounds and moves around me. I don't bother looking up at the tops of the buildings anymore. I just watch my feet as the sidewalk moves beneath them like a conveyor belt. I have a difficult time even seeing past my office window these days. I can't get my eyes to focus past the raccoon-eyed, pale-faced, haggard-looking stranger who absently gazes back at me from the reflection on the glass.

My hands automatically steer the car through curves that take me home at night, and they instinctively steer me back in the opposite direction when morning arrives again. My foot hits the gas pedal when my eyes register a green light or an open stretch of road on the parkway, and it presses down on the brake pedal when the red glow of traffic signals or brake lights strike my eyes, but my brain does not consciously participate. It is as if I've been watching my own body from a few feet behind. I've felt this way for months. Until this morning.

It was unusually bright on this Monday morning, almost as if my surroundings were intentionally pushing themselves into my consciousness, trying to wake my spirit from its slumber. As one of the Parkway's curves rushed toward me, I reached forward and touched the "Power" button on the car stereo, just to hear the radio tell me what my numbed senses had just begun to suspect:

"What a bright, beautiful day it is out there! Finally, a welcome break from the past few weeks of clouds and drizzle! So get out there and do something! We'll be right back after these messages, with noted anthropologist Doctor Hans Vetter, on Talk Radio ninety-eight point three . . ."

I gripped the wheel a little tighter, and a slight smile attempted to work its way onto my face. That's when the midnight-blue BMW came blasting past me in the right-hand lane, honking his horn and giving me the one-fingered salute through the open driver's-side window. He must have been going close to one-eighty. The BMW swooshed in front of me, just missing my front bumper.

"Asshole," I said.

His car raced ahead of mine as we approached the Bloor Street Viaduct, which hung across the Parkway with its black, riveted support arches looking like face-down crescent moons. The BMW rushed around the long curve ahead, then momentarily vanished in the shadow under the viaduct. As my car emerged from under the iron arch, I guess I must have seen the sea of motionless brake lights a second or two before he did.

I stomped on the brakes with both feet, and I held my breath as the trunk of my body lurched forward against the seat belt.

My sunglasses went flying from my face, breaking against the dashboard.

The screech of tires burned my eardrums and I watched the blue BMW swinging wildly back and forth on the pavement like it was trying to stop on ice . . . then that sickening, reverberant smack as the car crashed into the rear end of the orange cement truck.

My car came to rest no more than six feet from the back of the BMW. My head bounced back against the headrest, and the Mustang rocked from the sudden stop.

Just ahead of me, steam and smoke billowed skyward. Jagged hailstones of shattered glass rained down on the blacktop. Right beside my door, a wheel cover rattled like a quarter spinning on a tabletop.

Through the open window of the BMW hung the driver's arm, inside a navy-blue suit-jacket sleeve. Just below the white shirt cuff, the hand that had gestured at me only seconds earlier was open-fingered and motionless.

I sat inside the Mustang, unable to unlock my grip from the steering wheel, unable to exhale or even blink. The blazing glare of the sun made every detail of the scene more vivid than a nightmare. It was like when I was in grade five, and I tried on a pair of glasses for the first time, and immediately I saw all of the things that had been fuzzy and unrecognizable only seconds earlier.

The conversation being broadcast on the car radio seemed so loud, it was if the host and guest were conversing directly between my ears:

"And we're back with noted anthropologist Doctor Hans Vetter, on Talk Radio ninety-eight point three. Mr. Vetter is here with us today to talk about his new book, Wandering: The Primal Instinct for Human Travel. *Good morning, Doctor Vetter."*

"Good morning, Peter."

Noted anthropologist Doctor Hans Vetter had a voice which reminded me of what I imagined God's voice might sound like: gravelly, wizened, and slightly impatient.

The radio host asked, *"Could you tell us a little about the theory behind your new book?"*

"Well, the basic premise of the book," sighed Doctor Vetter, *"is that the current standard North American lifestyle exists in complete opposition to the way we're wired as human beings to normally behave. Historical, anthropological, and biological evidence suggests that human beings, as a species, are meant to wander from place to place, rather than 'putting down roots' and 'nesting' in one particular place, as contemporary jargon would have it."*

"Not good news for the condo developers then," chuckled the host.

Noted anthropologist Doctor Hans Vetter was clearly not amused.

"Those things are exactly the opposite of what the human spirit requires. Living in a tiny, one-windowed box, taking the subway or the bus or driving a car for six blocks, then climbing into a little box which whisks you up twenty-one floors and lets you off in another little box, this is all completely contrary to the appetites and desires of the human spirit."

I was suddenly feeling rather confined inside the cockpit of my black sports car. I released my grip on the steering wheel, and unfastened the seat belt which held me in. Others were also stepping out of their cars. Most were running towards the scene of the collision, towards the BMW, which looked as if it had choked to death trying to swallow the back end of the cement truck.

I took a couple of steps sideways, away from my car. I could still hear Doctor Hans Vetter's voice on the radio:

"Take, for example, the Masi tribe of Africa. If you imprison their warriors, the warriors die within days. There is none of the tragic separation between physical and mental and spiritual states which exists in North Americans; when a Masi is put in a box, when a Masi's movement comes to an end, then so does the Masi. And this is what is happening to many North Americans, only at a torturously slower pace."

Other commuters were standing around the BMW, peering through the window, alternately cupping their hands over open mouths, crying, screaming, or standing silently with their arms hanging slack at their sides.

"The idea of the human need for travel to inspire personal growth can be found in the words of the prophets and sages of all religions and cultures," the anthropologist on the radio continued. *"To quote Aitareya Brahmana, 'Living in the society of men, the best man becomes a sinner. Thus, Indra is the friend of the traveller. Therefore, wander!' Or, in Meister Eckhart's words, we must travel 'The Wayless Way, where the Sons of God lose themselves, and, at the same time, find themselves.' A proverb from India states, 'Life is a bridge. Cross over it, but build no house upon it.'"*

The guy in the blue BMW was only one car ahead of me. Those gawkers could have just as easily been looking at an only slightly different-looking dead man, in an only slightly different-looking navy blue suit jacket, in an only slightly different-looking sports car. They could have been looking at me.

"Gautama Buddha's last words to his disciples were, 'Walk on!'"

And now I am walking in the opposite direction that I was driving, through the frozen river of parked cars. The last words I hear from Dr. Hans Vetter, before striding out of the audible range of the car's speakers, are these:

"Even our own North American ancestors had it right. When a youth showed signs of restlessness, boredom, or disillusion, his family and friends would unanimously declare, 'Go west, young man! Go west!'"

I keep walking north, for a long time, until downtown is behind my back and the sun has fallen. Then, I turn towards the west.

Other than a quick, jittery stop at a bank machine to withdraw the daily maximum and stuff the roll of bills into my pocket, I have not been inside a box of any kind since I climbed out of my car on the parkway. I am not going back for my car. I am not going back to my apartment. I will not be showing up for work tomorrow morning.

I walk on, and I look up at the sky, which is now as vividly dark as it was bright this morning, and I notice the stars for the first time in a very long time. And it occurs to me that they are all moving, too.

PART TWO
The Rules of Attraction

"The meeting of two personalities
is like the contact of two chemical substances;
if there is any reaction, both are transformed."
—Carl Jung

The Jazz Man's Girl

They met on a dock on the last night of June.

He had played all night at the club just up the beach, and his sax was tucked in its case, which swung free in his right hand. The warm breeze dried the sweat on his brow, the sweat that made his top lip taste like salt. He had played hard, and he was tired, but it was that good, calm kind of tired.

Her black hair shone in the light of the moon. She heard the clip clop of his shoes on the boards, and she glanced up and said, "Hi there."

He stopped in his tracks.

"Hi," he said.

"You played at the club," she said. "You're good. You play like you mean it. You play as if there's a line from your heart to your horn."

The sound of her voice, paired with the beat of the waves as they slapped the pier, was just like jazz, and it made the hairs on the back of his neck stand up on end, like they did each time he played like he played this night, in that rare way that made the folks in the crowd hold their breath right up to the end of the song.

"Thanks," he said with a grin.

"What brings you here?" she asked. "Is it the wind, or the waves, or the songs of the gulls?"

"None of those things," he said.

His feet stopped right there, and he sat down at her side. She kicked with bare feet at the twin of the moon, which lay on top of the still lake's skin, and he had no choice but to take off his shoes and dip his toes in, too. Each splash of his feet made a ring, and each splash of her feet made a ring, too, and one by one, their rings touched and crossed through each other.

They talked 'til the small hours of the night, when at last he took her in his arms, and, as the sun rose once more in the sky, he said, "You're a lot like jazz, and that's not a bad thing."

She asked him, "Will you stay here with me, and play me a song?"

And stay he did. He took out his horn, and filled the night with song.

And he plays for her to this day.

Sky and Earth

(1)

I was born in a big city, and I live in a big city now. I have big city friends, and I spend my leisure hours doing big city things. But I make my living with charcoal stick, pencil, and paper, sketching portraits of ghosts of the rural past. I specialize in depictions of things that are either sprouting from the earth, or sinking into it.

My chosen occupation involves driving for hours, until paved roads are no longer optional, then I get out of my car and wander through retired farmlands until I find something: a water-warped plank in the darkened corner of a long-abandoned farmhouse, or a crusted leather glove, half-buried in dirt and bits of the last harvest's cornstalks, frozen in the middle of its decay. An old iron plough, perhaps, reddish-brown like the soil it once carved, flaking away in small measures, its return to the earth hastened with each rainfall.

I translate these scenes into two dimensions, solemnize them in shades of grey, isolate and sanctify them in frames of silver and black. Other city people pay me well for these sketches, which I sell within the vortex of the humming, swirling downtown art market. In an eight-by-eleven-inch frame, hung overtop a television set or a king-sized bed, things dead and decaying become pretty pictures. Death becomes a decoration.

Today is different, though. I am working on a type of sketch that I ordinarily never try. I am drawing a picture of a person, from memory.

My subject has a name, by the way. Her name is Robin, which suggests a little bird, flitting about, carefree, lighthearted, thoroughly unprotected. It is a name that is only about one-third correct in describing her.

I will begin by drawing her fingers. I remember her fingers more vividly than I can see my own, which grip this pencil like a lifeline. But at which point in time do I stop and draw? Which version of her fingers will give me the solace I need?

(2)

We are seven years old, exploring the landscape of Nana's farm. We are digging in the brittle grey dirt, our fingernails shearing the drought-baked crust like tiny steamshovel scoops. We unearth smooth, warm stones, bits of last season's cornstalks, bottle caps, shards of green and brown glass dulled and rounded at the edges by ages beneath the abrasive earth. Ants tickle our toes, the grass greens our knees, the sun reddens our cheeks and lightens Robin's hair to the colour of dried hay.

High above us, not much larger than the stars of the night, jet airplanes carve their signatures in the sky. Their vapour trails sit in the sky like white woolen strings.

Is this where I should stop and sketch?

Now it is the middle of July. We are thirteen, nearly fourteen, sitting cross-legged atop an old horse blanket, sheltered inside the musty stable, which has been free of horses for many years (though their odour still lingers in the spongy wood and straw).

Today we are explorers, brave and spartan, the first people to set foot on a newly discovered planet. This is the first time I have touched female flesh, and it is the first time that I have been touched this way by another.

Robin is soft and warm and malleable, in places where I am cool and hard and flat. She draws a vertical line upon me with her index finger, dividing me in half, starting at the pit of my neck, parting the soft tuft of hair which has appeared at the centre of my chest, stopping just millimetres above my belly button. She hesitates only for a moment, rests her face against my shoulder, then her fingers proceed with their descent. When she reaches the bottom of the trail, her other fingers join the lone explorer, and they curl up together like sleeping puppies.

She looks at me and smiles, her eyebrows cocked skyward. Robin is more brave in her explorations than I could ever be. She seems to have an instinct for this new territory, a natural understanding that I most desperately lack.

Her nipples are apple blossom pink, the texture of silk buttons on a grade-school teacher's blouse. I touch them lightly, with apprehension, as if my cool hands might destroy them, as early frost kills other delicate things. I am already too saturated, too overloaded with fascination to go any further than this, but Robin goes farther, causing the crooked walls to spin around me. My heart thumps like a ritual drum. Robin presses her face against my chest and absorbs my rhythm. I can feel her eyelashes twitch against my chest.

We move outside the stable, lean against its old, rough walls, our eyes rolled up at the sky. Airplane watching has become our equiv~ nt of stargazing, and I have learned to identify nearly any aircraft by the density of its vapour trail and the shape of its silhouette against the great dome of blue. At night, Robin can identify many stellar constellations, but I am the one who is most familiar with the sky's daytime inhabitants. I know more of the things which can be seen up close, touched, understood through mechanics, made with the hands. I know more of things that live close to the earth. Airplanes are as far as my mind ventures from the ground. The stars belong to Robin.

(3)

And now comes another scene, the one I want to draw, to capture and contain, to make trivial and small. But I cannot.

I am in the stable again, but the hazy air has given way to the cold clarity of winter. Robin is lying on her back on the hardened ground. There is snow and dirt in her hair, a rivulet of blood on her lower lip where a tooth has penetrated. Her skin is white from the cold, and she makes no sound. I can only be sure she is alive by the vapour from her breath.

On top of her is Danny, Nana's hired hand. His big hairy ass is bobbing up and down, obscuring Robin's waist. His chubby face is pressed against the side of a stall. Robin's thin white legs are pried apart by his own, his clay-crusted boots pin her ankles to the ground. Robin's dark eyes roll over in my direction, but she does not cry out. Her face displays no expression at all.

I have only now become aware of the predatory shriek that has exploded from inside me. My hand has wrapped itself around a handle which protrudes from a barrel of old farm tools, and the head of the sledgehammer has met decisively with the back of Danny's head before I am even fully aware of what I am doing.

He rolls over several times, legs kicking violently, his shattered skull sandwiched between his big bony elbows. His breathing becomes fast and shallow, like the breath of a hunting dog that's been shot by its master.

Robin is fully exposed now. Steam rises in wispy ribbons from her mouth. I take her by the shoulders, prop her limp body against the wall, pull her sweater down and her stockings up. I see the blood, feel the stony cold of her skin. He has ripped her winter skirt to ribbons trying to get to her, like a hungry scavenger might tear through a garbage bag for table scraps.

I am dizzy, the air in my lungs like molten metal. I lunge for the tool barrel, selecting another weapon. Both hands close around the handle, absorbing splinters as I raise it above my head and then plunge it downward.

There is a sound like plucking the stem from a ripe apricot as I skewer his belly with the prongs of the pitchfork. He screams with the rage and confusion of a colicky infant.

Shut up! Shut up! I jab him again and again, until his screaming is swallowed by the cold silence of the barn. His shirt glistens deep red, as from wine spilled on a tablecloth. Steam rises from the holes, disappears in the sterile cold. His blood pools thickly around him, penetrates the frost, is absorbed indifferently by the barren ground. Then, eyes wide open, his torso twisted like the trunk of an ancient tree, he twitches slightly in the warmth of his own death.

There are two parallel lines on Robin's face, frozen tracks of tears. She does not blink, or move, or make a single sound as I carry her across the field to the house. Clenched between her fingers are the ends of a thin, black cord. She has worn this cord for as long as I have known her. Danny has snapped the cord during his attack.

Danny. I have killed him.

Nana wraps Robin in blankets, sets her in front of the fire, calls a neighbour to retrieve Danny's body. I sit next to her for many hours, waiting for her to move or speak. Just as the flicker of the flames has nearly lulled me to sleep, I hear a faint utterance from her.

One word: "Wrong."

It's the last thing she says to me. Nana has both of us sent away before the end of the next day.

The paper crackles and resists, but I compress it into a tiny ball. It lets out a feeble death rattle as it settles into the wastebasket.

I don't think I can put this into a drawing.

(4)

Now I am six years old. My brother Michael is attempting to teach me how to hit a baseball with a bat.

"Ready, Philip?" he happily barks, like a Saturday-morning-cartoon bulldog.

"Ready, Mikey!" I chirp, thoroughly contented, knowing that Mikey is about to share another secret from his vast reservoir of eight-year-old wisdom.

"Remember to keep your eye on the ball!"

"Okay, Mikey!"

The ball sails over the plate, and lands softly in the grass behind me.

"C'mon, Philip! You didn't even swing! You were looking up in the sky! Whatsa matter with ya?"

"Sorry," I say automatically.

"Let's try again. Keep your eye on it. Here it comes."

Again, though, I am distracted by the sky. It is a beautiful, shooter-marble shade of blue, with subtle wisps of cloud penciled in fragile arcs across its great dome. Thin white trails, created from invisible air, clouds born from nothing, hanging weightless against an innocent blue, sketched by the glinting pinpoints. Jets. Airplanes. I love them.

"God, Phil! Another kid could've hit that ball with both eyes closed! With one arm tied behind his back! But you, you're too busy looking at the damn sky! Geeze!"

"Sorry, Mikey."

I start pouting, which is one of the few defense mechanisms I have. It is meant to remind Michael that he is the Big Brother, and that he has certain Big Brother responsibilities.

"Okay, okay, Philip, don't get all sucky on me. We'll try it again, okay?"

I continue to pout, sticking my lower lip out even further.

"Look Phil, we'll try again. You can hit the ball. You just have to concentrate."

"You'll yell at me!" I whine. This sort of thing really works on poor Mikey.

He walks over and puts his arm around me.

"I promise I won't yell at you, Philip. So whadda you say we try hitting that ball again! And tuck your lip back into your face, okay? A bird's gonna poop on it if you don't!"

We scamper back to our positions in the middle of the lawn.

I can still hear the jet planes moving quietly across the sky, but I watch the ball. I watch that stupid ball. I lock my gaze upon it, and, as it passes beside me, I hammer it with a whack that sends it flying nearly two yards.

Michael jumps up and down, cheering.

I look back up at the sky. There is a new vapour trail etched against the blue, one that hadn't been there before. One of life's great injustices: it is impossible to keep your eye on the ball and watch the sky at the same time.

"Stay right there, Philip," says Michael, as he runs towards the house, "I want Dad to see you hit the ball!"

My father is home today. This is very rare. His presence today lends a certain importance to anything we do.

(5)

Thomas Randall Skyler. My father. I didn't ever become familiar enough with him to think of him as "Dad." He was the inventor of several bits of apparatus that nobody has ever heard of, unless one happens to be a molecular biologist or a particle physicist. He built the prototype for a Stellar Mass Spectrometer, which is now standard equipment in university laboratories across the world, and his name is engraved on many other retired objects in lab closets everywhere: The Skyler Type 4 Mass Spectrometer, The Skyler Particle Analyzer, The Skyler-Branstrom Doppler Shift Compensation tables, and other items I can't remember, none of which I have ever really understood anyway.

Aside from being toolmaker to the Einsteins of his generation, however, my father had another little-known claim to fame. At age twenty-one, he was the youngest member of an elite group of scientists brought together during World War II for the purpose of isolating the most deadly neurotoxin that had ever existed. Information pertaining to this research is still Top Secret, but I know something about it just the same.

My father was working on his Ph.D. in physics at the time, and was recruited as a lab assistant by the group of scientists who were busy isolating the super-toxic compound known as Agent Z. He was involved in the actual scientific work to some extent, but in a very marginal way. When the toxin was finally produced and contained, my father was delegated to deliver the results to the National Research Council headquarters in Ottawa. They gave him enough money for an economy train ticket, three meals, and one night's stay in a Rideau Street hotel. They also handed him a briefcase containing a small plastic capsule that held about ten grams of Agent Z.

When my father arrived at the hotel it was quite late, and it was obvious that delivery of the substance would have to wait until morning, so he put the briefcase in the bathroom, opened the bathroom window, and shut the door behind him, just in case something happened to the capsule during the night.

That capsule of Agent Z, of course, when diffused through the air, was potent enough to kill every human being in the city of Ottawa. One bomb full of the stuff would have been enough to destroy the entire population of Germany—and my naive young father thought he was making himself safe by opening a window! The next day, he dropped off the briefcase at the designated NRC office, signed a release form, and was back at his post by that same evening.

My mother was eighteen years old and my father was forty-one when they married. She could barely remember World War II, and she was only vaguely aware of the conditions of my father's wartime work. Since the weapon had never been used, he naively assumed that all research pertaining to Agent Z had been destroyed.

At any rate, it was my father's name, and his name alone, which appeared on the release form that was stolen by a small group of radicals known as the "Action Front for the Elimination of Chemical, Biological, and Nuclear Weapons." They had a clever acronym, of course, as self-appointed vigilante groups often do: AFFECT BAN.

First came the threatening telephone calls, which demanded that my father give them the names of all the scientists who had worked on the project.

"Most of them are dead, and the rest are senile," he told them. "I'm the only one left, and I was never directly involved in the research. So forget about it. It's over."

But the calls continued. They demanded names, the locations of data, and other information that my father refused to give them. Our latest unlisted phone number would be in place no longer than three days before the calls from AFFECT BAN would begin again.

I can only vaguely remember the two military police that were posted to our house, and I remember nothing of the harassing phone calls that preceded their presence. I do remember what happened afterwards, though, when the calls stopped and the policemen went away.

(6)

Michael has just taught me how to hit a baseball with a bat, and he is running toward the house to get my father, so that my second hit will have the legitimacy which accompanies adult witness to a childhood milestone. Micheal is nearly to the steps of the front porch when it happens.

There is a package on our doorstep, which my mother, wearing one of her long, pastel-coloured dresses, has knelt to retrieve. The card, which will be later recovered from the eaves of our garage by the police detectives, reads: "To Doctor Thomas Skyler. With respect for all of your work."

My young, pretty mother is practically incinerated as the package explodes in her hands. The rush of flame consumes our front porch, and scorches the front of our house all the way to the roof. The demon roar shatters windows in neighbouring homes.

One of my mother's shoes is later found on the roof of a house two blocks away. Her wedding ring is embedded in the plaster of the living room wall.

I watch with burning eyes as Mikey is knocked onto his back by the shockwave; it is a small shockwave, I later learn, compared to that of an atomic weapon or even a conventional firebomb, but to me it is as if the Apocalypse has been unleashed in our front yard. The last thing I remember is Michael's wiry body bursting into flame, his screams, his blackening form writhing on the ground like a beetle on its back.

In my scrapbook, I have a clipping of the message that was sent out by AFFECT BAN to the larger city newspapers the next day. I received this small, three-column-inch message from an old yellowing newspaper, the type that some urbanites find charming to frame and hang in their dens. I bought the paper at the art market where I sell my sketches. This is what the clipping says:

AFFECT BAN (the Action Front for
the Elimination of Chemical, Biological, and Nuclear Weapons)
claims responsibility for yesterday's incident at the Skyler home.
The intended victim of the blast
was Dr. Skyler himself, not his
wife or any other member of his
family. Dr. Skyler was involved in
the manufacture of atrocious
experimental biological weapons
during WW2. This heinous knowledge cannot be left alive. We
regret the loss of Skyler's wife and
son, but we feel that nevertheless
another blow has been struck in
our battle to eliminate Chemical,
Biological, and Nuclear Weapons.

Apparently, though, AFFECT BAN didn't have a moral problem
with plastic explosives in plain brown wrappers.

(7)

My great-aunt Verna always insisted that we call her Nana. It is
a name that suited her well, I think—closer in origin to the
word "nurse" than to the word "mother." Nana provided good
physical care, but she was not what one would call a warm person. Nana's farm is located about fifteen kilometres from the
town of Faireville, which sits at the edge of Lake Erie, mostly
minding its own business. The nearest city could be on a planet
light-years away, for all the residents of Faireville know or care.
I was sent to school there, where I prayed every day to God (in
whom I still somehow believed) to take me away.

In His own peculiar way, God sent Robin to me instead.

She was small, she wore third-hand Salvation Army store clothing, and she had hair that made it look as if she was delivered to school each day inside a tornado funnel. In class, she spoke as little as I did, and the other kids ignored her equally at recess time. When I would wander to the back of the schoolyard, to camouflage myself in the thick mess of vines that had grown around the fence, it became her habit to follow me and sit beside me inside the vines. For the longest time we did not speak to each other, but I had to grudgingly admit that I enjoyed her silent company.

One day, while we were sitting together, dreading the ring of the bell that would end recess, she took hold of my hand. Her own hand was warm, like light from a fireplace, and the heat of her slight touch seemed to diffuse through my entire body.

"My name is Robin," she said quietly, in a clear, soft voice that perhaps nobody in the school had ever heard before. "I want to be your friend."

(8)

Halfway through the first year of our friendship, Robin was absent from school. I was worried. Robin was never kept home from school, even when she was sick.

"Class," our teacher said, "Robin's mother died last night. I think it would be a nice gesture if we all signed this card for her."

There were groans from a few of the kids in the class. I should have been angry, I should have wanted to hurt them, to punish them for failing to love Robin the way I did, but I was only puzzled by their reaction. Why couldn't they understand that it was not Robin's fault that she had been born the child of Winifred Bright?

Winifred Bright had lived in one of the apartments above one of the little stores in downtown Faireville. She had become an unwed mother at the age of sixteen, and thus became the Devil's Representative when the Sins of the Flesh were discussed in hushed tones by Faireville's tea-and-cookie social elite. Whenever the teenaged daughter of a town busybody was caught in the act of kissing a boy (or some similar atrocity), a finger would invariably be pointed in the direction of Winifred Bright, as an example of what happened to girls who distributed their affections indiscriminately.

I suppose Winifred eventually decided to play the role in which the townsfolk had cast her, because shortly after Robin was born she took to slinking down the sidewalk in plastic-wrap pants and loose, low-cut blouses that allowed for much jiggling and bouncing. She had the type of physique that inspired certain men, when they saw her, to lean out through the windows of their pickup trucks and hoot, "Whew-wee! Would'ja lookit THAT!"

Most of her time was spent atop a barstool in a dark corner of The Outpost, a windowless, stucco-splattered watering hole about two miles outside the town limits. Most non-clients referred to the bar as "The Outhouse," a fairly accurate moniker considering the clientele the bar attracted.

Winifred brought a man home from the bar nearly every night. According to rumour (nobody would ever admit to having discovered this first-hand), Winifred never demanded anything in exchange for a night in her bed.

"My love is free to anyone who needs it!" she would declare. In her own mind, Winifred was not a prostitute. She didn't ask to be paid for her sexual favours. Somehow, though, she managed to pay her rent, and feed and clothe her child, however meagrely, entirely with *gifts* from her many male *friends*.

Everybody in Faireville knew that Winifred had posters of Chairman Mao Tse Tung plastered all over the walls of her apartment. It wasn't that anyone had *been there*, mind you ... you could see them from the street at night. Winifred rarely bothered to pull her blinds down; some said that this was a clever

61

advertising technique. Her male *friends* would scratch their heads and wonder aloud just who in the world *Mousey Tongue* was. Her reported reply to such queries was this: "He's a man who says that we should all work together, that we should share our talents and our gifts with our fellow human beings."

It was Winifred's frequent habit to undress for bed in front of an open window, much to the delight of the boys who had quietly crawled out through their bedroom windows to carefully hide in the shadows of the small park across the street. She would lean through her window and sway back and forth, taunting the poor boys until their hearts were pounding as if tremors were shaking the earth. Then, when many of the boys were about to faint from lack of breathing, Winifred would finally unleash her enormous breasts from the confines of her lacy white bra. She would allow the invisible boys only the briefest glimpse of her famous possessions, then she would tug the blinds down.

Perhaps she really did believe that she was sharing her talents and gifts with her fellow human beings. Perhaps it was not until the moment she threw herself onto the rocks below Lion's Park Bridge that it occurred to her that she might be wrong, that she was being used rather than valued.

(9)

"But Philip," came Nana's flustered response to my desperate request, "I've never taken care of a little girl before! I wouldn't know what to do!"

"Nana!" I begged. "She has nowhere to stay! Please!"

Nana slowly shook her head. "I'm an old woman, Philip. I have a hard enough time looking after you!"

"But Nana!" I wailed. "They're going to send her to an institution!"

I'm not sure how I became aware of this, but I knew there was something in Nana's past that had given the word *institution* a meaning similar to *hell* in her vocabulary. I knew that she would not allow any human being to be sent to an institution if it was within her power to stop it. Nana was not wonderfully warm, but she was fiercely just.

"All right, Philip," she said quietly, displaying the tight-lipped frown which I later understood to be her version of a smile, "bring me the telephone."

Something about Nana changed at almost the same moment that Robin timidly stepped through her front door. Nana combed out Robin's tangled hair, washed her smeared face, and draped her in one of her own sweaters, which, on Robin, nearly touched the floor.

"You certainly are a pretty little thing, aren't you," Nana said. I had never heard Nana use a word like *pretty* before.

From that point on, there were uncontrollable bouts of silliness and laughter in Nana's home, and it became apparent to me that Nana was a woman who was full of love, but had never known how to show it until she was reminded that her hardened old shell had once been small and soft and pretty, too. All the love locked away inside Nana, once turned outward, was too much for just Robin and me, and she decided to hire several disadvantaged persons from town as live-in farm hands. Within two seasons, Nana's farm was transformed from weed-choked dormancy into the productive homestead it had been in its glory days.

Among the new faces at the farm was the round, red-cheeked mug of Danny Campbell, an ox of a man with the mental capabilities of a three-year-old. Danny could barely speak, and walked with an odd limp, but he was stronger than everyone else in our house combined. He had kept alive by doing heavy jobs for people around Faireville, accomplishing tasks that other townsfolk could not possibly do, for wages they would never accept. Although there was rarely anything more than an uncomprehending expression on poor Danny's face, I believe that he was much happier in the employ of Nana than at the mercy of the townsfolk, who saw him as something less than natural.

Nana saw Danny as someone who could be saved.

(10)

I have discarded half a sheath of sketch-papers now, but have yet to complete a single sketch of Robin, the way she was before we were torn apart.

I am running out of time. Tomorrow is Nana's funeral, and I know that Robin will be there.

(11)

Robin is wearing black, as I knew she would be, but I am stunned by how she looks. I expected that she would be shrunken, withered by trauma, but she is nothing of the sort. She looks sad, as one should look at the funeral of a loved one, but she is also slim, and tall, and incredibly beautiful. How odd it is that sadness is the detail which turns a pretty face into a beautiful one.

"Philip?" she says.

"Robin."

She takes hold of my hands and rushes all through me, like she has done every time we've ever touched. I have always been afraid of this power of hers. Despite the fact that I never really knew my mother, I have a very strong feeling that she had this same sort of effect on my father. This terrifies me.

The slim black cord is still around Robin's neck. A small knot holds it together where it was broken.

The funeral is soon over. Nana is safely tucked away beneath the crusted soil of her farm, which is once again overgrown with weeds, home to small wild creatures of many kinds. I am carrying my sketchpad. Robin is a few steps ahead of me. I am surprised that she has agreed to do this.

She leans back against the stable wall and exhales gently. My pencil makes slight scratching sounds against the paper, the only noises which dare penetrate the silence of this warm but solemn spring day. Robin toys with the knot of that slim cord, rolls it back and forth between her porcelain-doll fingers.

She asks, "Did I ever tell you about this cord?"

I shake my head.

"My mother gave me this necklace when I was very small. She used to wear it herself, before I was born. It's just a plastic string, really, but she liked the way it felt between her fingers. And she liked that it was never cold against her, the way gold and silver necklaces are."

I continue sketching. My mind is empty of words.

"I was wrong, you know," she says, as if I will know exactly what she means.

"Wrong about what?" I ask hoarsely.

She pauses, considering. "Remember when we used to come out here. We would touch and kiss, and try to talk about difficult things."

I look directly at her eyes, which I have not been able to do until now, and it has taken all the courage my weak heart can muster. "Yes. I remember."

"I thought that it was magic."

I am not sure what to say to this.

"I was wrong though," she says, to herself as much as to me. "I thought it was my magic. I thought it came from me."

She brings the knot up level with her eyes. "I thought I could make Danny better, if I shared my magic with him. But it wasn't my magic at all, and it didn't make him better, did it?"

I think about Danny, writhing on the ground in shock, like an animal that had just felt the hunter's bullet. "No. It didn't."

"It made him fierce," she whispers.

"It made him dead, too," I mutter, almost inaudibly.

(12)

There is nothing but the scratching of the pencil for an expanse of time.

Robin continues to fondle the knot in the cord around her neck.

"Love doesn't protect anyone from anything, does it?" she says, so abruptly that I drop the sketchpad.

I cannot exhale. Could this be the question I have been trying to force onto the safety of paper?

My father loved my mother and brother, but still they were destroyed along with him. Robin's mother loved anyone who asked her to, but still she was destroyed by them. I loved Robin, and Robin loved me.

I hold her around the waist. Our faces are wet with each other's tears.

Robin reaches to the pit of her neck and unties the knot in the cord. It drops to the ground as her arms pull me close to her again.

"Can we go on now?" she whispers in my ear.

We wander slowly away from the old stable, leaning against one another, eyes skyward. There is always an airplane in this vast expanse of sky.

My sketchpad is closed, nestled under my free arm, and the cord lies upon the cool ground at the place where it was first broken, left to be taken back by the earth.

Sandcastles, Waves

I have just told Madeline that the locals refer to this spot as *Splashdown Point*. She thinks the nickname is both cruel and clever.

Dozens of accidents have happened here. Another could occur at any time.

We are sitting together at the edge of a cliff, which rises above a stony beach. Madeline wanted to watch the sun set over the water, and this is the best sunset-watching spot I know of. This evening's sky has not disappointed.

Madeline touches my shoulder. "Here's a paradox for you," she says. "This sunset makes me feel small, but large, too. Next to it, I feel almost microscopic. But if I think of myself as a part of this . . ." (She throws her arms wide) ". . . I feel larger than life."

I think I understand. I can just as easily imagine this sunset overhead in Paradise as underfoot in Hell.

As if she can hear my thoughts, she leans over and whispers in my ear. "It all depends on your viewpoint, doesn't it?"

I watch our feet dangling over the cliff's edge. I can almost make myself believe that we are walking on air.

The warmth of her breath still lingers on my earlobe.

Less than a stone's throw from where we sit, there is a yellow-and-black checkerboard warning sign. It means exactly what it says: DEAD END. Every once in a while, someone sees the sign just a little too late; thus the nickname *Splashdown Point*. At least once a year, a motorist is lulled by a sunset such as this one. Then tires will screech. Metal will meet horribly with rock and shallow water. Glass will shatter. Flames will roar.

To be crushed, burned, or drowned. Madeline and I discuss which of these would be the least unattractive way of dying.

"If I had to die one of those ways," she says, in a ghost-story tone of voice, "it would be on impact. Blam! Crunch! Then it's over."

I myself would rather burn, flames roaring, a glorious blaze.

Madeline pokes my shoulder, says I'm a typical male.

We both agree that drowning would be the least preferable option.

On the beach, almost directly beneath our perch, Madeline notices an elaborate sandcastle, which somebody has built right at the water's edge.

"The wind is turning towards us," she observes. "Let's climb to the bottom of the cliff."

"Why?" I ask.

"I want to watch the lake take that sandcastle back," she says.

We hold hands on the way down, pretending that this will prevent us from slipping, secretly realizing that if one of us falls, we will fall together.

Earlier today, just after we arrived at my family's cottage, Madeline had a revelation: "Children live closer to the ground, don't they? They notice details which adults step right over."

She faded into herself for a moment, then suddenly burst forth. "I have an idea! Let's be who we were when we were kids! We can PLAY! We could even dress the way we did when we were children."

It seemed like a safe enough place to go.

So I made some cut-off shorts from my jeans with a fishing-knife, and I put an old pair of rubber boots. Madeline changed into her bathing suit, tied her shiny black hair into a ponytail, and left her wedding ring on top of the woodstove. (The wedding ring, incidentally, was given to her by someone other than me.)

We walked the beach like children would, Madeline skipping stones on the flat water, me sticking the toes of my rubber boots into the wet sand, still fascinated by the hollow sucking sound produced by the movement.

"Eleven skips!" shrieked Maddie.

The best I could do was seven.

Madeline and I could have easily been childhood buddies. Every girl I ever played with, dug in the sand with, hunted for frogs with, touched or kissed for the first or second time ... each one of these girls could have easily grown up to be Madeline.

Now it is later in the day, and we are adults again. We are on the beach at the foot of the cliff, standing beside the sandcastle. A tongue of water licks at one of its towers, then a larger wave takes a bite from its base. The tower tumbles, is devoured by the water.

Our shoulders are touching. I can feel Madeline radiating against me. She brushes a bug from my chest. Her slight touch is almost hallucinogenic.

Another tower crumbles into the surf.

"Cool," she whispers, facing me. Her lips hover dangerously close to mine for a moment.

Then, "Look," she shouts, "the castle!"

There is a smooth, shimmering stretch of sand where the castle once stood. Her voice drops to a whisper, the calm before the hurricane. "I guess there is nothing humans can build which nature can't break down. . ."

The waves lick at our ankles, and our feet, our knees, crumble beneath us. We tumble, we roll together in the shallow water, breathing each other's breath. Our tongues spiral together like opposing currents in an undertow.

Her lips, the pit at the base of her neck, the ridge where her ribcage meets her belly, the insides of her thighs, greasy from tanning lotion, smelling like coconut, tasting like salt.

The wet sand mirrors the deep-red sky, shimmers like a carpet of blood. The waves roll in, then away again, over and over and over, and only for this slender moment, our bodies understand.

Her flavour, her scent, the slippery oil on her skin, all carried away, dissolved in this cold crash of waves. The warmth of her mouth is the only haven in this swirling liquid tempest.

We could drown together in this moment. And maybe it's just the sound of my heartbeat thundering in my ears, but I am almost certain I can hear a car speeding towards the precipice above us.

The Sweeper

"**S**o then," he says, kneading one of her buttocks, "How 'bout a little treat for Daddy?"

"Goddammit, Larry," Carolyn grunts, turning. "You know I hate that 'Daddy' shit."

From behind her, Larry grinds his groin into the softness of her behind, and slides his fingers into the crotch of her panties.

"You know, Puddin,'" he whispers, "if you ever want to clearcut this bush, I'll be your lumberjack! Make you as smooth as a little girl."

She pulls away from him. "Christ! You're obsessed! Most guys go friggin' *freaky* for blonde pubic hair. It's supposed to be *rare*."

He begins unbuttoning her blouse, and it falls to the floor. Then, with one quick downward tug, he causes her breasts to spring free from her bra.

"If you really wanted to be rare," he says, "you'd have a *red* beaver."

She wrenches herself from his hold and turns away from him again, crossing her arms tightly across her breasts. She pretends to study her unsold paintings, which cover most of the flaking, discoloured wall.

Larry pushes his way between the paintings and Carolyn, and pouts in mock shame. A lock of dark hair falls into his face, which looks adorable, Carolyn admits to herself. Then, tossing his tie aside and slowly unbuttoning his custom-tailored shirt, he looks at her with those ice-blue eyes, and says, "Aw, come on, Puddin', you know I love you exactly the way you are."

With one fluid motion, he slides her skirt and panties down her legs, then rises and grips her buttocks in his hands. Her legs encircle him almost automatically, and he carries her over to the bed.

Damn it, she thinks, *I wonder how many other women he uses this Jedi Mind Trick on?*

But the thought drowns in the undertow as the swirling feeling begins.

Now Carolyn is lying on her side, tracing quaint circles in the small of Larry's back. God, the sex with him is great . . . and sometimes when he says, "I love you," he really sounds like he means it. Half the time he's so sweet—if only she could figure out how to tip that balance.

"What are you thinking right now?" she asks.

Usually, Larry is stupid enough to admit that he is thinking about how he would like to penetrate Carolyn while she's wearing a schoolgirl uniform, or how he thinks she would look waxed bald between her legs. It's a question that's led to dozens of apologetic messages on her answering machine.

This time, though, without the usual deliberation, Larry simply says, "Nothing. Nothing at all. Not thinking, only feeling."

Carolyn's fingers continue their whirlpool penetration, and she stretches across Larry on her baby-powder belly, and says, "Good answer."

Maybe he's changing, she muses.

Larry smirks into the pillow, thinking, *Leave it to a dork like Jeremy to come up with a great line like that one.*

The thought of Jeremy reminds Larry that the two of them are going out of town on business first thing in the morning. He can hardly wait. The adventure of the road! He shimmies out from underneath Carolyn, and says, "Gotta go, Puddin'. Business trip tomorrow."

Carolyn sits up in bed as Larry zips up his six-hundred-dollar suit pants, stuffs his feet into his shimmering shoes-of-the-week, and makes for the door.

"See ya in a week or so," he says, as he pulls his tie around his neck. Then he adds, almost as an afterthought, "I love you," and leaves the apartment for his own enormous house. Carolyn has never slept at Larry's house. For some reason, he prefers her dingy apartment for their encounters.

From her window, Carolyn watches Larry walk away through the alley with his thumbs hitched in his Italian leather belt, swaggering like a saddle-sore cowboy. She watches him round the corner of Wang's Chinese Restaurant in the direction of Main Street, where he parks his Corvette—Larry refuses to park it in the alley because of the dust.

Carolyn rests her forehead against the windowpane, presses her still-bare breasts against the coolness of the glass, feels her nipples turning to bullets, so hard they hurt.

"This is what you've become, Carolyn," she says to herself, "someone who can't tell the difference between pain and pleasure."

She closes her eyes and swallows hard, swaying her hips to the rhythm of the *swish, swish, swish* sound rising up from the alley. Then she jumps back from the window with a gasp.

"Shit! The crazy sweeper man!"

In the alley between her crumbling building and the back wall of Wang's Chinese Restaurant, a grey-faced stickman with a tattered straw broom swats away at the dust. The sweeper emerges late every night from the darkened doorway at the back of Wang's, which hides the stairs to the sweeper's single room above the restaurant. His room, Carolyn supposes, has the same view as hers: two dumpsters, a grease barrel, and a burned-out Chevette.

Swish, swish, swish.

Carolyn cups her left breast in her right hand, squishing the right one under her forearm, and places her left hand over her less-than-rare pubis. Thus covered, she tiptoes back to the window and peeks over the ledge into the alley. Usually she looks forward to watching the sweeper's nightly ritual, like others might wait for the tolling of church bells, but usually she is not naked.

Swish, swish, swish.

The crazy sweeper man is saying the same thing he always says, repeating it over and over again: "Dirty dirt, dirty dirt, can't chase it away, they track it back in, dirty dirt, dirty dirt, dirty dirt."

Swish, swish, swish.

"Does Larry really love me?" she wonders aloud. "I wish I knew for sure."

As she says these words, the sweeper stops sweeping and looks up at Carolyn's window, and despite the darkness she feels like he is looking her right in the eyes. A shiver goes through her body, and her skin is speckled with goosebumps. She backs away from the window.

Carolyn wriggles under the blankets on her bed, but, even in this summer humidity, she continues to shiver.

Jeremy sits in front of a bank of six huge computer screens, his spidery fingers typing madly. The doorbell rings, so he reaches for a different keyboard, taps a few keys, and a camera's eye view of his front step appears on one of the screens. It's Larry, carrying a portable computer under his arm. What could he possibly want at this late hour?

Larry's bravado makes Jeremy uncomfortable, but he somehow knows where to find these big corporate contracts, and he's good at convincing executives to pay a lot of money for computer system modifications which Larry himself doesn't have the slightest idea about. Jeremy, on the other hand, understands computers so well he practically speaks in binary.

"Whatcha doin' up at this hour, partner?" says Larry as he strides into Jeremy's house. "Jerkin' off to Internet porn?"

"I've, um, been, uh, working on the General Motors project."

"Oh. Good," Larry says. "So, you ready for the big trip tomorrow?"

Well, technically the answer is no, since Jeremy has been so busy programming that he's forgotten all about tomorrow's business excursion. But, since Jeremy can throw a bag together in five minutes or less, he answers, "Yes."

"Great! Um, say, bud, have you got an Internet line handy?"

"Yes," Jeremy says.

Larry shakes his head as he follows Jeremy through the foyer and down a long hallway. Despite Jeremy living in the place for almost a year now, the walls are still primer white, and, other than a few Froot Loops cereal boxes atop the refrigerator and some unwashed dishes in the kitchen sink, every room except Jeremy's bedroom is empty of anything other than drywall dust.

Jeremy's bedroom is a reassembly of his cluttered university dorm room. There is a rumpled futon in one corner, and overloaded bookshelves are stacked to the ceiling against one wall. There are several sheets of plywood on concrete blocks to provide desktop space for the half-dozen purring computers. On another plywood table, there is a neatly arranged display of what looks to Larry like junkyard salvage.

"What the hell is all this shit?" Larry asks.

"Oh, um, that's my Historical Computer Display. I've got a Texas Instruments TI99-4A, a VIC-20 and a Commodore 64, an

Apple II, a Radio Shack TRS-80—once known in many circles as the 'Trash 80.' And, look at this! A Timex Sinclair! Less memory than a modern scientific calculator. Bet you haven't seen one of these in a while!"

"Yeah. Thrilling. So where's that Internet connection? I need to make some arrangements for tomorrow night."

Jeremy plugs a cable into the back of Larry's notebook. Larry sits down on the lone chair in the room, turns on his machine and says, "Watch and learn, my friend."

Jeremy watches over Larry's shoulder as Larry logs onto an Internet site called onenighters.com. He reads aloud, " 'BigThruster,'—that's one of my online names—'Can't wait to meet up with you for some hot, pumpy fun when you come into town tomorrow night! I'm wet just thinking about it. Luv, FunnGrrl.'"

" 'Hot pumpy fun'?" Jeremy wonders aloud. "Do people actually talk like that?"

Larry ignores him, and reads aloud as he types, "FunnGrrl— Wear a schoolgirl outfit with a short skirt, and I'll teach you some 'lessons' you won't forget. Don't forget to shave everywhere!"

Larry logs off and closes his notebook.

"What about Carolyn?" Jeremy asks.

"Christ, Jeremy! What she doesn't know won't hurt her! And you better not say anything to her, 'cause I'll kick your ass."

"She'll find out herself," Jeremy says evenly. "Women are smart about these things."

"And how the hell would you know?" Larry grunts.

After Jeremy hears the tires of Larry's Corvette squealing away from the house, he opens a closet door and removes a watercolour painting, which he leans against a bookshelf. He sits down in front of the painting, cross-legged, and exhales slowly. It is a painting of Carolyn.

None of this would be happening if it hadn't been for Jeremy's sister. A while back, his sister had bumped into an old high school acquaintance named Carolyn, who mentioned that she had been having computer troubles. Playing Cupid as usual, Jeremy's sister immediately offered his assistance.

When Jeremy arrived at Carolyn's apartment, it occurred to him that her place was in some ways like his own bedroom: the futon bed, the shelves bursting with books, but with paintings everywhere instead of computer monitors. Cluttered, comfortable, and personal.

She was wearing loose, paint-splattered coveralls.

"Hi," she said, "Sorry I look so crappy. I'm doing a painting."

Jeremy thought Carolyn looked quite the opposite of crappy. In fact, she was so honest-to-goodness real-life pretty, he had a hard time looking directly at her. He examined her bookshelves instead.

"How did these books get this way?" he asked. "They look pregnant."

"Oh," she said, "The pages swell up when I read in the bathtub."

"You read in the tub?"

"It's the best way! In a bathtub brimming over with steaming water, with only my hands and face exposed to the cooler air. My body dissolves into the womblike warmth, and all that's left is my mind and the words."

Then she blushed. "Sorry. I babble. The artistic temperament, I guess."

"It's okay," Jeremy said, already in love. "I might try it sometime."

They stood there looking at each other, each smiling awkwardly, until Jeremy finally blurted out, "I'll, um, take your computer home with me. It needs a new motherboard, and, um, a few other little things to bring it up to date."

"How much will all this cost me?" she asked. "I'm not exactly getting rich from my paintings!"

"Maybe you could, um, trade me for one of your paintings," he offered, his heart rate increasing. "How about this one?"

"No, that one will never be worth anything. It's a self-portrait. It's only me."

Jeremy knew that, of course, and said, "Well, um, it's worth something to me, I think," and he gave her a strange, awkward grin.

To Carolyn, he looked like an alien from another planet trying to emulate a human smile. It made her feel a peculiar kind of warmth inside.

"Nah, it's ugly. I was in a bad mood when I did that one," she said. "Let me paint you something new. Anything you'd like."

"Another portrait of yourself," he said, his heart thumping wildly. "I mean, if that's not too weird."

"It's not too weird," she said.

She felt oddly aroused, even after Jeremy retreated from the apartment. She stumbled around for the rest of the afternoon with her head cocked to one side like a puzzled puppy, until eventually she filled her bathtub and climbed in, forgetting to bring a book along.

Jeremy devoted every ounce of his energy to rebuilding Carolyn's computer. He didn't sleep. He hardly ate. He didn't pause for anything, except to daydream about Carolyn. When he was finished, Carolyn's computer was ten times the machine it had been before—not that she would really ever know the difference.

Carolyn started, and then disposed of, four different paintings before finally finishing the one she would eventually give to Jeremy. In the first, she started painting herself wearing a long dress, with a sweater tied around her shoulders.

"Yuck! Hello, Miss Kindergarten teacher!"

She changed into a black skirt, tights, and a clingy black top.

"Oh, look, everybody! It's Miss Deep Dark Struggling Artiste."

As she looked around the apartment for something else to wear, she caught a glimpse of her naked torso in the mirror, and she imagined the look on Jeremy's face as he removed this version of herself from its brown paper wrapping. It gave her a shiver, and a tight little smile crept onto her face. She had only applied a few brush strokes when she removed the rest of her clothing and started again.

When she finally stepped back from the finished painting, her pulse was racing like she'd just sprinted up five flights of stairs.

"I'll drop by in a few minutes to pick up the computer, and to drop myself off to you," she said over the phone. "Er, the self-portrait, I mean!"

Jeremy scrambled around the house, tossing junk into the empty closets, then bagging up used paper plates, pizza boxes, some junk mail and a couple of uncashed cheques, delivering it all to the curb.

She had that warm, fluttery, weird feeling inside her again. It was almost frightening to feel this way. She had been living alone for so long.

She set the painting down against the bank of computers, then she ran the tip of her finger along the spine of every book she could reach.

"Too perfect, too uncreased, too unread-looking," she whispered, more to the books than to Jeremy. Behind her, Carolyn could hear the paper being unwrapped from around the painting, and she missed the reaction she had been waiting for.

"I like the expression on your face in this painting," Jeremy said. "It's like you're looking into the future."

"These books look brand new," Carolyn said, facing the bookshelf, still unable to turn towards him. "How is it that a man can leave books so ... unchanged?"

Jeremy walked out of the room.

Oh no! Carolyn thought, *I've insulted him!*

But Jeremy soon returned, holding out a softcover novel, which was swollen and misshapen from absorbing bathtub steam.

"I read your way, now," he said, showing that strange alien grin again.

And that was when Jeremy's business partner Larry came crashing through the door, acting like a normal horny earth-man, flirting, hovering, undressing Carolyn with his eyes. Within twenty minutes, Larry had talked Carolyn into going on a date with him. Larry wouldn't take no for an answer, and Jeremy had just stood there and let it happen.

And that was that. Jeremy sighed, shrugged, and returned to his computers, forbidding himself to feel anything but ambivalence.

Three nights have passed since Larry left on his business trip, and he hasn't called Carolyn yet, so at first she thinks she's dreaming when the phone rings sometime after three AM. She punches at the "speaker phone" button on her bedside phone, but hits the professionally done picture of Larry he's left there, accidentally breaking the glass. Fully awake now, she jabs the phone button on the second try.

"Hey, Puddin,'" Larry squawks through the speaker.

"Larry ... why the hell haven't you ..."

"Look, baby, Daddy's been kinda busy arranging a whole lotta computer fixits fer ol' Jeremy to take care of. And also I forgot to bring the charger for my cell phone. Just bought a new one today!"

"A new charger?"

"No, a new cell phone! Hell, with the dough we're gonna make on this deal, we could..."

"Larry, are you drunk? It's late..."

There is some noise in the background.

"Larry, is there someone there with you?"

"No! Nobody's here!"

The sound of stifled giggling can be heard in the background.

"Who the hell is that giggling, Larry? Jeremy?"

"No. No! You didn't let me finish. There's nobody here . . . but my client! I'm having a meeting with my client."

"At three AM?"

"We've had a *lot* of things to discuss. . ."

More giggling in the background.

"Shit!" Larry yelps, "The phone is flashing! I think the battery's about to go dead. I'll. . ."

There is a beep, and Larry's voice abruptly stops.

A clever ruse, thinks Larry, who shuts off the cell phone so Carolyn will be unable to call back.

A very young woman, no more than nineteen years old, is stretched out in front of Larry like nothing he could have ever pictured while she was still inside her waitress uniform. Each line, each curve, each shadow of her glistening, sun-bronzed body seems to quake, to shimmer like rain beneath a streetlight. Those long, wiry muscles in her arms, stretched tight as high-voltage wires in winter, her cheeks, her chin, the strip of bedsheet that covers her breasts like a clue in a riddle, the expanse of milk-smooth belly which rises from the liquid shadow, it all leaps forth and strikes the eye like laser light, like revelation.

Damn, thinks Larry, *there is nothing more intoxicating than getting away with it.*

"I will *never* forget this body," he says to her. He forgets her name at the moment, but he can reach down to the floor for her nametag if the need arises.

In his drunken, aroused state, Larry does not realize that he pushed the number 3 button on the phone, rather than the *end* button.

Carolyn sits up in her bed and listens to the speaker phone as Larry says, "Now it's my turn to ride *you*, Chiquita!", followed by the sound of squeaking bedsprings, and flesh slapping against flesh.

Carolyn knows she should be boiling over with rage, but she only feels numb and tired. She shuts off the speaker phone, then gingerly plucks Larry's photo from its shattered frame, noticing for the first time that her hand is bleeding. She walks over to the window with the photo, tearing Larry's picture neatly in half, then into quarters, and eventually into bloodstained smithereens.

With her uninjured hand, Carolyn pushes the window open.

Outside in the alley, the stickman sweeper is chanting, *dirty dirt, dirty dirt, it won't go away.*

"You've got that right, pal," Carolyn says. She flings the Larry-fragments out into the air, blood from her cut hand spattering the windowsill, and says, "Larry, I wish you would just disappear."

The stick man stops sweeping, watches as the shreds of photograph twirl towards the ground like dying moths. Then, despite the near impossibility of him seeing her through the darkness, Carolyn again feels his eyes lock with hers, and again she feels that strange chill ripple through her body.

"Messy," the sweeper says, "messy."

She looks away, muttering, "I wish I could find a good man for a change."

The words have just passed her lips when there is a knock at the door. She opens it without thinking twice.

It is Jeremy. He is out of breath and soaked from perspiration, looking like he's just come in from the rain.

"Jesus!" he says. "Your hand!"

Carolyn holds her hand up in front of her face. Liquid vines of crimson twist around her forearm, drip onto the floor.

Jeremy catches her as she passes out.

When she comes to, Carolyn is wearing her comfy pajamas. Her hand in wrapped snugly in bandages. She is on her bed, leaning against Jeremy's chest. Jeremy is bigger than she thought he was. It's like he was hiding inside a smaller version of himself until now.

"My self-portrait," Carolyn says, "Do you still have it?"

"I keep it hidden in a closet so Larry won't know I have it."

Jeremy expects Carolyn to be relieved, but she looks disappointed.

"Oh," she says. "I see."

"I . . . I take it out at night, though. I fall asleep looking at it."

Carolyn's lips part slightly.

"It makes me dream about you," Jeremy says.

Carolyn closes her eyes. "I think I wished for you tonight."

They kiss. It is a kiss that erases every kiss Carolyn has ever shared, and every kiss Jeremy has ever imagined.

"I'm not working with Larry any more," Jeremy says. "I took the train home, and I walked here from the train station."

"That's at least two kilometres!"

"I ran, actually. I needed to see you. There are some things you need to know. . ."

Carolyn sighs, and snuggles against Jeremy.

"I already know. He screws other women. A few nights ago, I wished to know whether he really loved me or not, and tonight I found out."

"Geeze," says Jeremy, "Do you have a wishing well or something?"

Outside the window, there is a faint *swish, swish, swish.*

"Or something," she says.

Larry is speeding through the city with the convertible top down when he spots a group of young girls walking along the sidewalk: short plaid school skirts, knee-high socks, blossoming breasts, long fawnish legs.

As he drives past, he cranes his neck to get a longer look.

"Man! I love 'em at that age!" he brays.

He looks ahead just in time to see the parked mail truck. With screeching tires, he barely misses it. The back end of the car slides sideways, and the Corvette careens to the right, down a side street, roaring and spinning on the gravel, downhill towards an abandoned pier. His fashionable leather-soled shoe jams beneath the brake pedal at the worst possible moment for Larry.

Bubbles gurgle on the surface of the deep, black water. Larry, attached to the sinking Corvette by his right foot, disappears from sight.

The police dial the number of Carolyn's apartment, which is one of many on a list they retrieve from Larry's wallet, but there is no answer. She has already put her clothing in Jeremy's empty dressers, and has hung her art on the walls. Jeremy reads to her in a tub full of warm water, in what is now their house. They intertwine, surrounded in steamy warmth, both believing they can see into the future.

Bloody Tourists

They lie side by side on their backs, two great, fleshy mounds rising out of the white sand, their sunscreen-slathered skins burnt red in the afternoon Cuban sun.

"Pearly-Pearl, this is just like being in Heaven."

"Danny-Dan, this is Heaven. It's truly magic."

Pearly-Pearl giggles when Danny-Dan reaches over and slaps her thigh, sending ripples through her loose skin like a stone dropped into stagnant water. He reaches behind his head, one man-breast rolling back to reveal a strip of glowing white skin that hasn't yet been scorched by the intense sunlight, and he tugs an extra-large insulated mug from the sand. The pail-sized mug, which in bright pink lettering reads "PARTY NAKIDD!!!!" was brought from home to maximize the resort's All-You-Can-Drink policy.

"Damn!" says Danny-Dan, after loudly gurgling the dregs of his drink in his straw, "all outta happy juice!"

He rolls over on his side to stand up, when Pearly-Pearl chirps, "Don't bother getting up, hun! That waitress is *finally* heading over this way."

Danny-Dan settles onto his back again, waves the empty cup in the air, and calls out, "Yo! Señorita! El thirsto over here!"

"Two more Cuba Libre, señor?" says the waitress as she kneels to pick up their special mugs.

"Nah, just bring me two more rum 'n' Cokes," says Danny-Dan, slyly positioning himself to get a better view up her skirt. "And if you get back here fast enough, there's a good tip in it for you."

"Yes, señor," the waitress says.

"It took her so long to come back over here, she doesn't deserve a cent," Pearly-Pearl hisses, peering haughtily over the rims of her plastic sunglasses as the waitress trots along the boardwalk to the beach bar. "Look at the hussy way she sways her butt when she walks! Thinks she's J-Lo or something."

As his wife rambles on about the waitress's visible panty line as if it's a festering, cancerous boil, Danny-Dan spies a shapely woman walking along the shoreline from a distance, and his heart rate increases when he realizes that she is wearing only a bikini bottom. He gropes wildly for his digital camera.

"Hey, honey-buns," he says, "lemme snap a few pics of you with that beautiful ocean in the background."

"Okay!" Pearly-Pearl says brightly, rolling over and smiling for the camera.

"No, no, sweets. Look away, like you just were. Sexier that way."

As soon as Pearly-Pearl turns away again, he extends the zoom lens and frantically snaps a dozen pictures of the topless young woman.

"How'd they turn out?" Pearly-Pearl wonders. "Let me see!"

"Ah, not so good," Danny-Dan sighs. "My fault—wrong settings. I'll delete them."

By pressing a few buttons, he hides the photos away in a sub-folder inside the digital camera, so he can later reacquaint himself with the young woman's breasts when he has a moment alone in the hotel room bathroom. Danny-Dan then spots another woman in the distance—not topless, but with an equally attractive figure.

"Hey, Pearly, look! It's Princess Stephanie! And Roger-Dodger."

Pearly-Pearl and Danny-Dan sit up and wave enthusiastically.

Roger and Stephanie walk side-by-side along the beach, scouting for a couple of beach chairs, most of which are unoccupied but have been claimed with towels, by tourists Roger assumes are currently clustered inside the 24-hour buffet, inhaling their seventh meal of the day.

"You know, Steph," Roger says, shaking his head, "compared to Centro Habana, this place feels about as authentic as Disneyland."

"Oh, lighten up," she says. "Look how pretty the ocean is."

"Okay, sure, but ... *shit!* Quick, Steph, turn around!"

"What?"

"Too late," Roger sighs, "they've already seen us."

Stephanie squints into the blazing sunlight.

"Who?"

"The Bovines, that's who."

"The *Devines*," Stephanie corrects him.

"I'd call them the *Warthogs*, but it doesn't rhyme. Bloody tourists!"

"Roger, we're also tourists."

"Steph, we're *travellers*. Those idiots are *tourists*. They're the reason that Cubans and people of other struggling cultures have such a poor impression of North Americans. Fat, stupid, drunken, all-you-can-eat consumerist pigs."

"Roger!"

"Why didn't we ask them which resort they were staying at in Varadero, so we could move to another one? Or, better yet, why didn't they just stay home in Dorkville, Ontario, and spend the week waddling back and forth from their mini-van to the all-you-can-eat buffet at their local pancake house?"

Stephanie jabs him in the ribs with her elbow. "You promised you would be nice."

"Fine," Roger sighs, and he waves half-heartedly at the two round figures that flap their arms at them from a distance. "There. Now let's go the other way."

"Rog, have some manners. We have to at least go over and say hello."

"Fine," Roger grumbles, "but if that Dan guy calls me Roger-Dodger one more time, I swear I'm going to kick sand in his moustache!"

Pearly-Pearl and Danny-Dan meet them halfway, both lugging enormous mugs full of rum and cola.

"Hey, Roger-Dodger! Princess Stephanie!" Danny-Dan calls out to them, hoisting his mug in the air, "Been getting your share o' the free hooch?"

"Well, no, we just arrived here this afternoon," Stephanie says, "but we did buy some excellent seven-year-old rum at a little distillery in Havana just before we left."

"Why the hell did ya buy booze, when it's all included for free here at the resort?" Danny-Dan brays.

Despite Danny-Dan's dark sunglasses, Stephanie can tell that his eyes have been aimed at her breasts the entire time, but she decides she doesn't care. *My boobs look great in this bathing suit,* she thinks. *At least someone's noticing them.*

Just a few nights earlier, in their room at the Hotel Nacional, Stephanie had stretched out on one of the double beds, wearing only the translucent panties that used to drive Roger wild with desire, but he remained crouched over his laptop on the adjacent bed, tapping away at his Havana article. Before this past December, when Roger was declared a runner-up in the feature article category at the National Periodical Awards, he would have been on top of her within seconds; now the only thing that seems to raise Roger's pulse is chasing that elusive first-prize story.

Danny-Dan is confused by Stephanie's sudden silence. He hopes he hasn't offended her. He pries his gaze from her breasts and turns to Roger.

"Hey, Roger-Dodger, did ya drink the place dry? Damn, rum's cheaper than water in this country. Betcha coulda bought the whole damn distillery with your credit card, eh?"

"Ha ha!" Roger says, "We're not all high rollers like you car dealers, Dan!"

"Call me Danny-Dan, Roger-Dodger!"

That Danny-Dan had inherited a car dealership from his late father was one of the many personal facts he and Pearly-Pearl had shared with Roger and Stephanie as both couples bounced around inside the shuttle bus from Jose Marti Airport. Roger and Stephanie were stopping at the Hotel Nacional for five days in Havana, while the other couple would continue on to an all-inclusive resort in Varadero for the full week.

"Havana?" Danny-Dan had wondered loudly. "Why the hell would you wanna go to that crumbling old heap of a city, when you could go to an sparkling-new resort right on the beach? It's all-inclusive, ya know, all the food you can eat, all the booze you can drink."

"And none of that pesky reality, eh?" Roger muttered to himself.

"Actually," Stephanie offered, "we're going to spend the last two days of our vacation at a resort in Varadero, so we can at least get a couple of days on the beach."

"Two days don't sound like no holiday to me," said Danny-Dan.

"Well," Roger sighed, "I'm also writing an article on the way that Havana's architecture reflects its various historical eras, contrasting the excesses of the Spanish colonial era and the Batista years with the Soviet-inspired austerity of the Castro regime. So I suppose we're mixing a little business and..."

"You're a writer?" Pearly-Pearl suddenly interrupted. "Do you think you could help me get my poems published?"

"Well, um, probably not. I'm a newspaper columnist, so I wouldn't really have much influence in..."

"I'm a prize-winning poet, you know!" Pearly-Pearl beamed. "In high school I won third prize in the Faireville County Fair Poetry Contest. I got my poem published in the *Faireville Gleaner* and everything."

"Well," Roger said in a businesslike tone, "be sure to mention your publishing history to any prospective publishers, and I'm sure that..."

"Wow, Danny-Dan! A real writer, sitting right here next to us!"

Danny-Dan frowned. "Hey, Roger. What kind of car have you got? You can tell a lot about a man by the kind of car he drives."

"We don't own a car, actually. My office is a seven-minute walk from our condo."

"We live and work in downtown Toronto," Stephanie added, "so we take the subway or we just hail a cab. We don't really need a car."

Danny-Dan pondered this for a moment. "But what if you wanna leave the city?"

"Then we rent a car," Roger said.

"Oh. I see. Rent a car. Sure." His voice rose. "Well, me, I can drive pretty near any damn car I want to. I'm Dan Devine, AKA Danny-Dan, the Car Dealin' Man, owner of the biggest car dealership in Faireville, Ontario."

Danny-Dan didn't receive the glow of recognition he expected from Roger and Stephanie.

"I bet you've seen our commercials on TV—'Devine Chrysler

Dodge, Where the Deals are Devine'? They always put a little halo over my head at the end of the commercial."

"Sorry, no," Roger said.

"Maybe they don't show that channel in Toronto," Stephanie added.

"Well, anyway, that's me. Danny-Dan, the Car Dealin' Man. At your service, ma'am. That's what I always say in the commercials."

He leaned forward and took Stephanie's hand, kissing it.

"From now on I'm gonna call you Princess Stephanie, 'cause you sure look like a princess to me."

Roger struggled to keep from rolling his eyes.

Pearly-Pearl looked like she was trying to burn holes in the back of Danny-Dan's head with her glare. "Danny inherited the dealership when his daddy passed on," she said evenly. "His brother Bobby does most of the actual business. Dan's more of, uh, what does Bob call it? A figurehead. He gets to be in the commercials, and wear the cowboy hat."

Danny-Dan slumped back into his seat, and said nothing for nearly a full minute. Roger gave a silent prayer of thanks.

And so they meet again, on this beach in Varadero.

"So, Dan, er, Danny-Dan," Roger says, "That's quite a hat you're wearing. I see it matches your big mug."

"Yup," Danny-Dan says, grinning that special kind of grin that only the combined effects of inebriation, dehydration, and sunstroke can produce. "It's part of a 'Beachside Party Pak' we picked up at the local dollar store. Two-for-one sale, so Pearly got one, too. It came with these sunglasses, too. All of the stuff says 'PARTY NAKIDD!!!!' on it, which is my personal philosophy right now, 'cause, hey, you're in Jamaica, right, mon? Who knows ya here, right? You can get naked if you want to, eh mon!"

"We're in Cuba, honey," Pearly-Pearl giggles. "Jamaica was last year."

"Ah, whatever," Danny-Dan burbles. He leans on Roger's shoulder, pointing up the beach to the topless woman he had photographed earlier, who is now lying on her back on a lounge chair.

"See? Lookit her. She doesn't give a shit. She wants to feel some sun on her tits, so, hey, she's lettin' em out. We should all just let it all hang out. Who cares! It's Jamaica, right?"

"Cuba, Danny," Pearly-Pearl reminds him.

"Er, well, Dan, that woman's obviously got breast implants," Roger says. "Women with fake breasts don't tend to be so shy about exposing them. It's more like pulling the cover off a Corvette than exposing a private part, I think."

"I've driven Corvettes," Danny-Dan says, glancing at Stephanie. Then he remembers his original train of thought. "Come on, kids! It's Ja...Cuba. It's Cuba! Who cares about anything? Let it all out!"

Pearly-Pearl unties the straps of her bikini. It drops onto the sand, and her small, conical breasts spring out from her round body. Roger tries not to look, but the two vanilla-ice-cream-white triangles against a crimson-sunburned background are about as subtle to the eye as car headlights bursting suddenly through fog.

"Just like this, Danny-Dan?" Pearly-Pearl titters, wiggling her cast-off bikini on the end of her big toe.

"Yeah, just like that, baby," he says. "Now how about you, Princess Stephanie?"

As if Roger hadn't seen that one coming from across the ocean. As if those dark sunglasses had concealed that Danny-Dan's eyes had been scanning Stephanie's body the whole time.

"But I'm wearing a one-piece, Danny,' Stephanie stammers, "so really, I don't think..."

"Just take the whole damn thing off, then. It's Ja ... Cuba! Who cares!"

Stephanie blushes, takes a step backward.

"Actually," Roger says tightly, "we were about to go into the ocean for a swim. For hygienic reasons it's best to keep one's bathing suit on. Even in Ja-Cuba."

Roger takes Stephanie's hand and steps toward the ocean.

"Hey, mind if I join you kids?" Danny-Dan wonders. "I haven't been in the water all week. Pearly's afraid of sharks."

"Oh, don't worry," Roger says to Pearl, unable to stifle a chuckle, "this water is way too warm for sharks. You've seen *Jaws* too many times, I think."

"Well," Pearly-Pearl says, "if a *journalist* says so, then I believe it." She reties her bikini top around her thick torso. "I'm coming, too."

Pearly-Pearl giggles the whole time she's in the water. "I've never been in the ocean before. It's so warm! It's so blue! It's so easy to float in! It's truly magic!"

"Or it's warm because the sun's rays shine more directly at this latitude, and it's blue because of the reflection of the Caribbean sky, and also because of the lack of phytoplankton, which is what causes the greenish tint to which we're more accustomed in North America, and it's easy to float in because the high salinity increases the water's buoyancy. But it could also be magic, I guess."

Stephanie gives Roger a look that tells him yet again to *be nice.*

Danny-Dan, who has been holding his gut in, lets it out again once it is safely submerged. He splashes around Stephanie the whole time, like a big, dumb dog.

"Well," says Stephanie after a few minutes of wading around in Danny-Dan's wake, "that was enough to cool me off. I think I'll go in for a drink now."

"Hey, let me buy the first round," Danny-Dan jokes, wading out of the ocean behind Stephanie, his vision locked onto her Stairmaster-toned buttocks, which flex from side to side as she strides toward the shore.

When she is out of the water from the knees up, Stephanie calls out to Roger's head, which appears to bob on the water's surface, "Are you coming, too, sweetie?"

Stephanie is wearing her white bathing suit. When it's wet,

you can faintly see her red gumdrop nipples, and, if you look closely enough, her sparse patch of blonde pubic hair. Roger knows that Danny-Dan is surely looking closely enough; he must be about to spontaneously combust.

"Nah," Roger says sweetly, "I think I'll enjoy the ocean and all its magic for a little while longer. But you two have fun!"

Facing Roger, Stephanie pushes her sunglasses up her nose with her middle finger.

Pearly-Pearl wades toward Roger and giggles, "I'm staying in, too. I might never leave the water, ever!"

Stephanie says, "You two have fun, too! We'll see you later."

At least she gets to have some booze, Roger thinks.

"Hey, Roger," Pearly-Pearl says, "while it's just the two of us out here, maybe you'd like to hear my prize-winning poem?"

Oh, good lord, thinks Roger, *please, anything but that.*

"Sure," he smiles, "let's hear it."

"Okay, well, I know it's not perfect, and that my work needs a good editor and all that, and that I've never had any formal writing training, and that nobody reads poetry anyway and I'm never going to get famous at it, and..."

"I'm listening, Pearl."

"Well, okay. Here it is. 'Stop.' By Pearl Devine."

She takes a deep breath, and recites:

stop

speak softly, brother
and carry nothing but questions

unclench your right hand
left hand
lips, teeth

exhale
be still, don't even breathe

feel
the earth tug
at your soles, the
musky air settle on
your skin, saturate
your brittle bones

no answers
will you hear
but you will feel your
place

Roger is silent. The sounds of the ocean seem more vivid than just seconds earlier. Roger floats quietly in the blood-warm water, relaxed, letting the salty water carry him.

"Oh, you think it sucks, don't you," Pearly-Pearl wails. "What an idiot I am. Here I am, all desperate to have a real writer tell me that some stupid poem that got published in a stupid local newspaper, some stupid poem that came in third to a couple of poems written by some other small-town loser hicks, that my stupid poem is somehow. . ."

Her voice trails off.

"It's a good poem, Pearl," Roger finally says.

"Really?"

"Really."

"Well, I was never sure if it was really any good or not, because the judge for the poetry contest was Mizz Appleby, one of the church ladies, and I always figured she picked my poem for third prize because she thought it was about God or something. The poems that won first and second prize were those 'Jesus Loves Me' rhyming-type poems, so I always wondered if Mizz Appleby would have picked mine at all if she'd known that mine is just about being open to the beauty of your surroundings. So I thought maybe if you, a real writer, liked it, then maybe it wasn't a mistake, and maybe. . ."

"Listen, Pearl. If your other poems are as good as that one, I've got a friend in the newspaper business who edits for a small press as a side gig. Maybe I can hook you up with her."

Pearl squeals and throws her arms around Roger, and his head plunges under the water. He bursts through the surface again, coughing, spitting salty water.

"Sorry about that," Pearl says. "Why don't we go join Stephanie and Danny-Dan at the beach bar. I feel like celebrating!" She blasts out of the water and shuffles through the sand to the beach bar, unaware that Roger is not following her.

Roger floats in the water, breathing slowly, and time becomes irrelevant. He listens to the calming rush of the waves breaking, feels the warm water trickle from his ears, watches the sun gently tuck itself into the horizon, feels the light turn orange then red on his face. Eventually he wades slowly toward shore in the last light of the day.

By this time, the beach bar has been transformed into a nightclub, which pulses with coloured light and throbs with sound. Roger orders a drink at the bar and wanders over to where Danny-Dan, Pearly-Pearl and Stephanie are congregated around a table.

"Hey, Roger-Dodger!" Danny-Dan calls out, "You totally missed seafood night at the buffet! I musta eaten three dozen mussels!"

"Where have you been for so long?" Stephanie asks, sucking down a margarita. "Working on your article in our room?"

"I was floating in the ocean."

"For so long? Sheeesh!" Stephanie always says sheesh after she's consumed a certain amount of alcohol.

By popular demand, the four-piece electric band plays "Guantanamera," albeit a quick-tempo disco version of it. Roger figures that Cuban bands must be about as sick of requests for "Guantanamera" as North American bar bands are of "Brown Eyed Girl" and "Born To Be Wild."

"Oooh, I love this song," Pearl squeals, and she grabs Stephanie by the hand. "Come on, sister!"

"*One ton o' mayo!*" Danny-Dan sings along, "*I ate-a one ton o' mayo!* Good one, eh Roger-Dodger?"

"You'll be the next Weird Al Yankovic," Roger says.

As Danny-Dan settles into the chair beside him, Stephanie glances back at Roger.

"Wanna come dance with me, husband?" she says, in that cute cheerleader tone of voice she gets when she's drunk.

"Maybe when they play a slow one."

"Sheesh!" she says, and she bounds out onto the dance floor with Pearl.

There is an awkward silence between the two men.

"So what's that you're drinkin' there, pardner?" Danny-Dan finally says.

"A mojito."

"Looks kinda like a girly drink, with all them leaves 'n' stuff floatin' around in there."

"I assure you, it's no girly drink. Ernest Hemingway loved them. They're especially good with five-year-old amber rum, rather than the moonshine they dump into the drinks at this place."

"Well, shut me up, then," says Danny-Dan. He waves his hand in the air for a waitress. "Hola, señorita! Bring us two mosquitoes, with five-year-old rum."

"He means mojitos," Roger adds.

"Amber rum cost extra, sir," the waitress informs Danny-Dan.

Roger expects him to kick up a big fuss about everything supposedly being *all-inclusive*, but instead Danny-Dan hands her a ten-peso note, and says, "Keep the change, señorita."

As their wives dance to another fast song, the two men each have another mojito. Another fast song, another mojito. And so on.

"Y'know, Roger Dodger," Danny-Dan says, his eyes glassy,

"we've only known each other for a week, but it feels like a lot longer than that."

"Well, actually, Dan, it's really only been a few hours in total. Forty minutes or so on the shuttle bus into Havana, less than an hour swimming in the ocean, another hour drinking at this place."

"Well, anyway, I feel like I know you well enough that I can tell you somethin' personal. Can I tell you somethin' personal?"

"Oh, I don't know if that's really..."

"Listen, I think Stephanie, your wife ... man, she is about the most beautiful thing I have ever seen in my whole damn life. You are one lucky man, brother. Damn."

Roger looks out onto the dance floor, where Stephanie is bouncing and swaying to the music. And laughing with Pearly-Pearl. Laughter, smiles, and kindness come so easily to Stephanie, no matter who she's with. She's always telling him to *be nice,* as if being nice is as easy for an ordinary human being as it is for her. Roger watches her the same way that Danny-Dan has been watching her all day. And he is right about one thing: Stephanie is the most beautiful thing Roger has ever seen in his whole damn life.

"You're right," Roger says to Danny-Dan, "I'm lucky to have her."

Tonight, back in their hotel room, he will turn off the air conditioning and throw open the windows, let that fragrant, warm air rush right in, just like it did the first time, when he and Stephanie were seniors in high school and her parents were away for the weekend. He will savour every inch of her just like he did then, kissing and touching and holding each curve, each little crevice, each stretch of goosebump-speckled skin, with his eyes wide open, absorbing every detail so he might remember it forever. He will discover her for the first time again.

"But," Roger says, clinking his mojito glass against Danny-Dan's, "you're a lucky man, too, Dan. Pearl is a real poet. You should encourage her. You should coax that beauty inside her to come out."

Danny-Dan nods his head slowly.

"These mojitos sure are tasty," he says. "I thought they looked like some gay yuppie drink, but I'm glad you got me to try one."

The band starts into a slow song, a Spanish-sounding number that Roger hasn't heard before.

"I'm going to go dance with my wife now," Roger says.

"Well, I reckon I'll go dance with mine, too," says Danny-Dan.

As they turn slow circles together, Roger unclenches his right hand, his left hand, his lips, his teeth. He closes his eyes and holds Stephanie close, feeling her goodness radiate into him, and for the first time in ages, Roger feels his place.

Reasons

Maybe I love you because you love thunderstorms and backlit sunset clouds like small apocalypses.

Maybe I love you because you leave dandelions tied to my doorknob, strings of jute from the frayed spot on your backpack tied to the light over the kitchen table, and blossoms to dry like artifacts atop my computer screen.

Maybe I love you because your name means Princess and mine means King (and the implications of meaning are priceless).

Or maybe I love you because you like walking through golf courses in the middle of the night (but not during the day, because of the plague of golfers then).

Maybe I love you because you were born in the same month as I, and when we're together we mesh like two gears with identical teeth. We spin in such a way that we are really never sure which one is doing the driving and which one is being driven, and maybe I love you because all this makes me think that perhaps astrology is not such complete bunk as I once thought it was, since we were born under the same sign, and, when you think of things that way, distance and time don't matter so much.

Maybe I love you because you could be sitting on your bed right now, waist-deep in a warm shallow pond of blankets in a swirl around your waist and legs, like waves which have paused for breath. You could be supporting a notebook on your round white dimpled knees, writing a poem to give to me tomorrow, when you sneak into my house for an hour or two.

Maybe I love you because you sometimes let yourself in to my house when I'm not even there, with the spare key I keep hidden behind the door on a nail. You leave cookie crumbs and funny notes behind for when I get home and you've already left, and I put them safely away, like parchment quotations from long-lost sages (the notes, not the crumbs).

Or maybe I love you because you eat your cupcakes from the bottom up, saving the sweetest part for last, waiting for that final burst of icing-sugar sweetness to melt slowly in your mouth, like the way I am waiting for you to stay for a whole night sometime.

Maybe I love you because we once bought two goldfish together, and you took them into the mall washroom and held them between your legs as you sat, and for the first time I felt jealous of fish in a plastic bag. Maybe I also love you because you picked stones from the beach with me, inspecting each one as if it were an opal or a tiger eye, condemning to the brownish water those judged less than unique, and later you held our fish flipping in your bare hands as I arranged those pebbles at the bottom of the tank.

Maybe I love you because of the bittersweet smell you leave behind on the armrest of my well-travelled couch when you fall asleep waiting for me to come home.

Maybe I love you because you and I are both slender and tall like reeds in a pond, reeds which bend in the same direction as the breeze is inclined to sway us.

Maybe I love you because of the way your small perfect breast fits perfectly into the cleft in my chest when we dance, and maybe I love you because we are even dancing like this at all, because we have to kill the lights and pull the shades, because you are supposed to be somewhere else.

Maybe I love you because of the ring my grandmother gave to me, saying "Save this for your princess, when she comes." It was made from one of the diamond earrings Grandpa had made for their twenty-fifth year together, a symbol of the greatest love I've ever seen between two people, until maybe now. You once tried it on, and it fit like a birthmark, and if I don't someday give it to you, I will probably give it to no one at all.

Or maybe I love you because you left your rings on the beach one night (including my grandmother's ring, which became yours the first time you put it on), and it was I who found them and gave them back to you again.

Or maybe I love you just because you found me.

PART THREE
The Power of Destiny

"But the power of destiny is something awesome;
neither wealth, nor Ares, nor a tower,
nor dark-hulled ships might escape it."
—Sophocles

Destiny's Telescope

Look at the stars. Billions of them. From our position up here, they all look pretty much the same. Specks of white. Inconsequential pinpoints.

Of course, we know better than to believe only what we see. As we zoom in closer, towards just one of these tiny points of light, we are reminded that every star is unique. No two are alike in composition, size, or colour. Each has its own potential.

And, if we turn our lens into the blackness that fills the space between these tiny, glowing specks, we can see that it really isn't as completely empty as it appears from a distance. There are nearly imperceptible bits of dust, thin traces of gas, invisible waves of magnetic current, charged particles which jitter frantically through the void, and other flecks of wayward debris—stuff that could have become stars but, for one reason or another, didn't make it.

Of course, we already know all of this without even looking. We can feel everything that is going on out there. But we will look anyway, just to remind ourselves that our duties lie in these little details.

Let's zoom in even further, adjust the fine focus on our mighty scope, pick out of the darkness a tiny sphere. This sphere is difficult to see, because it is so tiny, and half of it is always dark. But, on the side currently illuminated by a nearby star, we are able to see something unfolding, something which may ask for our involvement. We *are* Destiny, after all, and there is always work to do.

If we crank the magnification knob as far back as it will go, if we fine-tune the lens and squint really hard, we can see a wisp of beach, and two long, thin shadows extending from two small individuals who are stretched out on the sand. One of these figures is male, and the other is female. They are human beings. Their small planet turns gradually away from the ordinary yellow star around which it orbits, and the tiny place they occupy is about to turn away from the star's light. They call this *watching the sun set.*

The male is lying on his back, his torso twisted slightly to one side, his head propped up by one arm. The female is lying parallel to the male, in a similar pose. They are facing each other, talking.

The image in our lens is so tiny, so heavily magnified, that we will have to use some imagination. We must try to see things from the perspective of these two small beings. The sky that surrounds them is soft and pastel pink, and the backlit clouds stand boldly in the sky, mountains of vapour. The two are almost overwhelmed by it. If only we could show them the beautiful things *we* know of! Nevertheless, this is the kind of surrounding that inspires large topics of conversation in these small beings, and it is from this perspective that we will investigate.

Let us observe.

The male is speaking to the female.

"Look. Nobody is predestined to do anything, and nothing lasts forever. My actions and decisions help funnel and shape the course of my destiny. And the repercussions of my actions erode me, rebuild me, and make me into something new. That's how destiny works, I think. And that's why I don't try to force it. Destiny will do what it's supposed to do."

(We smile. They always come within inches of understanding us, but one of our inches is one of their light years.)

The female responds. "Hm. Sounds like you've given this a lot of thought. Of course, it's also a convenient excuse for doing nothing, if you don't mind me saying so."

The male laughs. "I don't mind you saying so, but I think you're missing my point. Things will happen whether you want them to or not. Nothing is certain. Nothing is guaranteed."

"But shouldn't you try to *make* things happen the way you want them to?"

"Sometimes we don't realize that we want something to happen until after it happens. That's why it's better to just wander forth, and let things fall into place as they will."

This does not please the female, but she tries to sound less agitated than she feels. "You're making excuses. You just want to justify not taking responsibility for anything, not making any sort of commitment. I don't think destiny will work for you unless you work for it."

(We shake our heads again—another inch the size of a universe.)

The male sighs. "Responsibilities are the repercussions of the things a person does. How can I put this. . .they are the echoes of actions. You don't wake up one day and say 'today I'm going to be responsible.' Responsibilities either happen, or they don't. You don't *take them on*, as the popular expression goes. They take on *you*."

He is pleased with himself, and lies back on the sand.

Time passes, and their planet turns a few more degrees away

from the sun, darkening their sky. The male looks over his shoulder at the glittering wall of downtown skyscrapers, longing to be downtown, wandering up Yonge Street with her hand in his, navigating through the buzzing summer crowds, absorbing the smells of street sausages and french fries, the sounds of honking horns and throbbing music, the electricity of the city at night.

The female stares ahead at the spot where their star disappeared from view, submerged beneath the line between sky and earth. She sighs, and decides that the time has come to drop the big issue into the conversation, the issue that has been lurking in the shadows of every word spoken so far.

Almost whispering, she asks, "So you don't believe in marriage, then?"

He pauses. He knows he has to get this just right.

"When two destinies run parallel, and seem likely to continue that way," he says, "I suppose marriage is alright."

She raises an eyebrow. "It means you have made a commitment. Is that what you mean?"

"It means a commitment has *happened* to you, I suppose."

She settles back against his chest, and her wispy hair, crisp and dry from a full day of wind and sun, blows against his face. He enjoys this feeling of contact with her more than he can express with words, so he says nothing.

(This saddens and frustrates us ... they are so close to setting us to work! Will neither make the necessary first move?)

Much time passes before anything else is said. The male has been nearly lulled to sleep by the rhythmic rush of waves upon the beach, and, at first, he thinks he is dreaming when she says something, very quietly.

"So do you love me, or not?"

The words ripple over her lips, no louder than a breath, but he hears them like cannon blasts. For the first time, he detects her pain, that this discussion has been more than just academic to her.

He sits up, and puts his arms around her. "Yes. I love you. I've loved you since the day I met you."

Tears begin to roll down over the gentle terrain of her face. She does not want this to happen, but it happens. She can already hear his answer to the question she is about to ask.

"Okay," she says, stiffening her lips, "You love me now. I know it. I feel it. But will you love me forever? Or will destiny change that whenever it feels like it?"

He clears his throat, pauses. He sighs, and pauses again. "Oh, I don't know. I wish I did, but I don't. Anything could happen between now and forever. There are no guarantees in life. I'm sorry, but there aren't."

She buries her face in his shirt, and can feel her tears soaking through. He wishes he could have simply told her that, yes, he would love her until the end of time. But his greatest trait and his most tragic flaw are one and the same: he is honest. If there is even a remote chance that a promise will not be kept, he will not make the promise.

"I love you *now*," he says. "Why isn't that enough?"

We turn our lens away from the two of them for a moment, because neither has done anything to activate our energies. When this moment passes, so will this moment's potential. If only there was some way to let them know.

Sadly, we turn the lens of our mighty scope away from this scene. We turn our attention elsewhere, knowing exactly the things which could have blossomed between them.

We crank back the course-focus knob of our great scope, and the tiny world shrinks into the illusion of blackness, hidden in one of the dark expanses between stars. We notice that bits of interstellar matter are slowly struggling towards a single point in one of these dark spaces. They are hoping to come together, to collide, compress, and start a chain reaction of friction and heat and gravity, which will cause them to eventually become a star.

But gravity fails. There is nearly enough friction and heat, but not enough matter has risked itself for the reaction.

The star dies, unborn.

Good Deeds

It's nearly midnight on Christmas Eve, and Barney Gundt has just finished eating his turkey roll dinner special at a local place called The Paradise Diner. In silence Barney finishes his coffee, scoops up the last smudge of pumpkin pie filling with the edge of the fork, and pauses to watch the snowflakes turn pink in the light of the neon sign humming just outside the dust-coated window. Then Barney puts on his earmuffs and scarf, buttons up his trusty old overcoat, and leaves a tip for the waitress on the tabletop.

"Have a good evening, hon," the waitress calls after him. No *Merry Christmas*, no *Happy New Year.* The waitress already knows Barney's story, and Barney knows hers, so the traditional holiday greetings are respectfully avoided.

"Yes," Barney says, "thank you."

The bells above the doorway jingle. Jingle bells. *There's no escaping it,* Barney thinks.

Outside, the snow is falling in big, fluffy flakes, illuminated like falling stars by the streetlights. The air is crisp and cold and still, as if the whole city has paused to hold its breath. Barney pauses to hold the frigid air in his lungs for a moment, to let a few plump snowflakes melt on his cheeks. Then he continues trudging toward the intersection, his head down, the fresh snow crunching beneath his boots.

Barney can faintly hear "Have Yourself a Merry Little Christmas" echoing from a loudspeaker outside a department store a block away.

"Martha's favourite Christmas song," Barney says to himself.

"Ahhhhh," says the homeless man at Barney's feet, "pretty song."

Barney is startled. Like many other lifetime city dwellers, Barney has become used to people huddled under blankets on the sidewalk, like he is used to the screeching of streetcar wheels and the night-time glow of streetlights; mere features of the urban landscape.

Barney looks down at the grizzled man sitting atop the warmth of a subway grate, then reaches into his front pocket and drops a five-dollar bill into the vagrant's paper coffee cup. It's Christmas Eve, after all. Better to give than to receive, right?

"Thank you kindly, sir," the grizzled man rasps.

The street signal changes from DON'T WALK to WALK, but Barney is motionless, his face frozen in an expression half sentimental, half pained.

"Martha used to say that all the time," Barney finally says. "I'd help her put the turkey in the oven, or take a turn whipping the mashed potatoes, and she'd say, 'Thank you kindly, sir.'"

"Hm," grunts the man on the subway grate.

I always gave her help when she needed it, Barney tells himself. *So I lost my temper once in a while, raised my voice. But, on balance, I was a pretty good husband. I did more good things than bad.*

Barney's expression brightens.

"Wait right here, my good man!" Barney chirps.

"Not goin' nowhere," the homeless man wheezes.

Some time later, Barney returns to the street corner with a box marked 'Paradise Diner.'

"Christmas dinner," Barney says as he kneels in front of the homeless man. "Turkey roll, mashed potatoes, corn, and turnip, all with gravy almost as good as Martha's used to be."

"Ummmmmm," says the man on the grate as he opens the box, inhaling the tendrils of fragrant steam.

Barney discreetly puts the plastic cutlery back into his coat pocket as the homeless man begins scooping the hot food into his mouth with his fingers.

"Mmmmmm!" the man on the grate groans as he devours the dinner.

Barney used to make similar noises as he dug into Martha's annual Christmas feast, which of course had real turkey, not turkey roll, and gravy made from the drippings, not this stuff out of a can. And Martha's desserts!

Barney wonders, *if a person does more good than harm, he gets to go to Heaven, right? This ought to count as a good deed. This should bring me a step closer.* Barney is unsure of the rules of Heaven; he often teased Martha about attending church every Sunday, and on the rare occasions that he accompanied her, he usually drifted into sleep before the sermon was half finished.

"I'll be back," Barney says to the homeless man, as he turns on his heels and marches back toward the restaurant. He returns a few minutes later, grinning like a little boy.

"Wasn't sure if you preferred apple or pumpkin pie, so here's both. And coffee, too. I ordered it double-double, the way I like it. Hope that's okay."

Barney hands over the warm coffee cup and fragrant box full of pie. The homeless man tucks into the apple pie, then the pumpkin, moaning slightly as he gobbles down the sweet desserts. Licking his fingers, the man on the subway grate starts to say something, but Barney raises his hand.

"Don't thank me," Barney says, feeling strangely lightweight, almost vaporous, as if he is hovering just outside of himself. *One more check mark in the Good Deeds Column for me,* he thinks. *I'm on my way, Martha.*

"Have Yourself a Merry Little Christmas" plays again from the loudspeaker up the street.

"From now on your troubles will be out of sight," the homeless man sings, in a surprisingly rich baritone. "My favourite, too."

"Farewell, my good man," Barney says.

The homeless man watches Barney turn away and step from the curb onto the deserted street. Then he hears Barney gasp, clutch at his chest, fall face-first onto the snow-covered pavement, with one arm folded under himself, his legs and other arm splayed out from his body at odd angles, like a discarded marionette. One of Barney's cheeks is pressed into the snow, and a single wisp of steam rises from his crooked lips, spirals gently, then vanishes in the crisp air. Snowflakes collect in Barney's silver hair and in the folds of his coat, and they melt and trickle down his motionless face. This is what the homeless man sees.

What Barney himself sees is something quite different. He does not see the homeless man shaking him to try to wake him, nor the waitress crouching in the snow feeling his wrist for a pulse. The only thing Barney sees is the one person he has seen every day for the past three years in his memories and dreams.

"I've come to you, Martha," he says to her.

"Thank you kindly, sir," she replies.

As he reaches out to touch her, she disappears, replaced by stars rushing toward him from a deep black void. Barney is sure he hears Martha calling out, "Stay with us, Barney," but he can't see her, there is nothing to grab on to, she's slipping away.

"Martha! Martha!" he cries, and his lungs fill with cold, dry winter air. The stars are really just falling snowflakes, lit up by the streetlights. The waitress, who has been giving Barney CPR, says, "Stay with us, Barney, stay with us."

Barney gasps, sits upright, tears and melting snow soaking his face.

"God, Barney," the waitress pants, "I thought I'd lost my best customer."

The homeless man laughs, claps him on the back and says, "You didn't think you could get away that easy, didjya?"

Barney sits silent and motionless in the middle of the road, with the waitress and the homeless man crouched beside him. The snow falls harder now, the sticky flakes gradually turning their clothes white, the three figures fading into the snow-blanched surroundings, becoming almost invisible.

"Barney?" the waitress whispers, "you okay?"

The department store loudspeaker is playing a different carol now: "There's really no place to go, Let it snow, let it snow, let it snow..."

Softly, Barney repeats the lyrics, "There's really no place to go."

Black Taxi

ADVENTURE THERAPY

Gil Raphael is draped over a molded-plastic chair in the cavernous foyer of the newly contructed twelve-theatre movie house in the heart of the Entertainment District. He examines his reflection in the wall of windows beside him. Inside this first-run Hollywood-blockbuster multiplex, the glaring fluorescent lights emphasize the dark circles beneath his eyes.

"I'm thirty-one and I look eighty-five," he mutters to himself, as he watches his reflection swirl the remaining swig of Leffe Blonde around the bowl of its stemmed glass. "I look like the living dead."

Sighing, he glances around the interior of this colossus. Huge flat-screen televisions hanging everywhere. Neon tubes flickering, strobe lights and mirror balls blinking, whirling spotlights slashing randomly though the air. Video games bleeping and chirping nearby, and hidden speakers booming melody-free bass notes at chest-thumping volume. *It's as if this place was designed by an eight-year-old with Attention Deficit Disorder on a three-can Coca-Cola high,* Gil muses.

Western culture, Gil thinks, *it's already crashed, in a digitally animated explosion.* He rolls his eyes upward, only to be confronted by an enormous model of the TV *Starship Enterprise* hanging from the ceiling, bow-to-bow with a *Klingon Warbird.* It annoys him that a few bytes of his precious brain capacity are being eaten up by knowing the trademarked names of these two big plastic things, and he is even more perturbed that they've named this loud, bright indoor carnival of name-brand consumerism after a classic old-style cinema. Gil longs for the formal dignity of theatres built in the 'forties, with their ornate high ceilings and red-carpeted foyers, velvet stage curtains and stylish light fixtures. *The Capitol, The Paradise, The Regent, The Palace,* all reduced now to crumbling, third-run repertory houses, or transformed into halls for wedding receptions and bar mitzvahs, or boarded up and awaiting the wrecking ball, to be transformed into Starbucks and Baby Gap generica.

Two teens on Rollerblades skate past, oblivious to the flashing and rumbling, making Gil feel even older, more obsolete.

He looks at his watch. *What the hell is keeping her this time?*

Gil thanks goodness for this bar area, cordoned off from the rest of the teenage circus with a rail of chromed steel. Gil takes his last swallow of the sweet, strong beer, and looks back at the window, past the reflections this time, out into the city, where the shadows of the summer evening are stretching towards night. The windows in the surrounding buildings become speckled with lights, and the after-hours version of the city begins to come alive.

A million things happening out there, Gil muses. *What the hell am I doing in here?*

From just behind the chrome railing, a voice chirps, "Hiya, sweetie cakes!"

It's Melissa, bouncing on the toes of her pink jogging shoes, fitting seamlessly into the neon and noise. She's wearing her usual figure-hugging spandex, a sleeveless black bodysuit this time, with stripes of pink drawing the eye from her almost mathematically conical breasts to the V of her crotch. The clingy material leaves few details of her young, athletic body to the imagination. Her pink sneakers match the brightest colour of spandex on her body; it's Melissa's fashion trademark. The first time Gil had sex with Melissa at her apartment, the pile of running shoes spilling out of her closet reminded him of a knocked-over jar of fruit-flavoured jelly beans.

Gil's heart rate increases. "Hello, Melissa," he says, wiping the pink-sparkle lipstick from his mouth.

"*Missy*, silly," she teases. "Maybe when I'm as old as *you* people can start calling me Melissa, *Gilchrist*!"

"Never call me Gilchrist," Gil says as he steps over the railing. "My parents should have been charged with cruel and unusual punishment when they named me that."

"*Gil* is cool, though," Missy says cheerfully as the two begin walking toward the entrance to the dozen movie theatres

"Yup," he says, placing a hand on her behind, enjoying the feeling of her tight cheeks flexing as she walks almost as much as he enjoys the envious glares from the young and older men alike. "Gil *is* cool."

Any woman Gil's own age would have immediately swatted his hand away, hissed that people were *watching*, but Missy doesn't even seem to notice.

Gil feels young and alive again. He likes to think of this as *The New Era of Gil. Gil, Revised and Updated. Gil, Reborn.* Gil's past five girlfriends, six including Missy, have been much younger than him. When one of few remaining friends from his university days meets Gil's latest belle, they sigh and say things like, "Gil, you ol' dog," or "Whatever keeps you young, buddy," but their wives are more blunt, use words like *cradle robber* and *dirty old man.*

121

"The movie's probably already started," Gil says to Missy. "Why so late?"

"Oh. I had a client pop in at the last minute to schedule an appointment. You know how it is in my business."

Missy's "business" is "Adventure Therapy." Gil can't make himself say or think the term without mentally placing quotation marks around it. Well-to-do Bay Street businessmen pay Missy by the hour to take them camping, rock climbing, mountain biking, and so on, with the added bonus of getting to watch her fit young body flex and stretch and bounce around in contour-gripping spandex. Gil pats her almost impossibly perfect behind, and thinks, *who can blame 'em, really?*

‡

Gil met Missy at the Mountain Equipment Co-op store on King West, where Gil was looking for a new pair of sunglasses. Missy's arms were full with a couple of pairs of hiking shoes, a backpack, and several skimpy spandex outfits, each specially designed for cycling, climbing, canoeing, or whatever. It wasn't the impressive terrain beneath Missy's tight athletic clothing that caught Gil's eye, though—there were dozens of pert, young, athletic women around the Co-op, both customers and staff. What pulled Gil to her was that, from a distance, Gil thought Missy looked a lot like someone he had once known.

"Melody?" He gasped when she appeared from behind a display of mountain-climbing ropes and hooks. *What was Melody doing back here in the city? Why hadn't he heard from her? Was she still with* him? The questions came in a dizzying rush.

"Melody!" he shouted out to her.

Missy, startled, dropped a pair of hiking shoes. When she bent over to pick them up, the rest of her purchases tumbled out of her arms and onto the floor.

Gil scurried over to help her.

"Sorry," he said sheepishly, "you reminded me of someone I used to know."

"I've heard that line before," she smiled. "But I'll let you buy me lunch anyway if you come up with something better."

Gil was about to insist that, really, she looked just like a woman he used to be in love with, but he realized how lame that would sound. Besides, crouched down face-to-face, he discovered that she really didn't look much like Melody at all. Her features were sharper, her blonde hair straighter and a shade darker than Melody's, and Melody was more of a flowy-skirt kind of dresser—she would never wear jelly-bean-coloured spandex like the woman crouched before him. Gil intended to mutter an apology, hand her stuff back to her and scurry away, but that impulse reversed itself in less than a second when she batted her eyes at him.

"Wow," he said, "are those coloured contact lenses or something?"

"Nope," she said, rising to her feet. "One hundred per cent real." She lightly ran her hands over her yellow-clad torso. "Just like the rest of me!"

Gil stumbled slightly as he sprang to his full height, still clutching her athletic gear to his chest.

"Your eyes," he said, "damn—that colour. A little darker than the ocean by a West Indies beach, a little lighter than those little blue flowers that grow on the side of the mountains near Lake Louise. I've only seen that colour once before."

"Okay, okay!" she said, "You can buy me lunch!"

Gil knew that Missy had to be at least ten years his junior, but his brain was temporarily overwhelmed by those incredible eyes of hers (and, he had to admit, her spandex-clad body may have had some influence as well).

Gil took her to an expensive little *haute cuisine* restaurant tucked away in an alley in the Annex, which he knew served delicious game meats, complex, refined appetizers and desserts, and, best of all, had a fantastic wine list. Missy ordered a cheeseburger and a Budweiser, neither of which were on the menu, then claimed that the goat's cheese on the burger tasted funny, and that the premium beer she was given instead of the Bud Lite she ordered tasted skunky. As Missy babbled on and on about new and popular bands and movies and Internet sites Gil couldn't have cared less about, he suddenly felt like an out-of-touch, middle-aged dad taking his daughter out for lunch after her first year away at university.

When Missy excused herself to go to the washroom, Gil decided to pay the bill and escape before he started feeling the need to go shopping for walking canes and adult diapers. But Missy returned before the waiter had brought Gil's credit card back.

"You're awful quiet all of sudden," Missy observed.

Gil squirmed.

"Look, Missy, it's been fun having lunch with you, but . . ."

He tried to avoid them, but her eyes locked onto his and started tugging him closer.

"Look, Gil, it's cool, okay?" she said. "I like my men to be a little older than me. I've never been one for *boys.*"

Gil averted his eyes from hers, only to find himself staring at her firm, round breasts, her tiny nipples straining against the yellow spandex.

"I've got the rest of the day off," she said. "Why don't you come back to my apartment and hang out a while?"

She reached across the table, lightly brushed his forearm with her fingertips. The hairs stood on end. Other parts of him reacted similarly.

"I think we might be able to find something in common if we try."

They spent the rest of the afternoon at Missy's claustrophobic one-room loft near the dance-club district. She didn't have an air conditioner, and Missy's futon bed was soon soaked with their sweat. During Round Three—and this was what sex with the energetic, athletic Missy was like for Gil—she straddled him, her hands on his shoulders, grinding his back and hips into the sheets. Her damp hair clung to her sharp cheekbones, her face defined by the daylight filtered through the dust-coated skylight. Spasms ran through Gil's body, and he let out an anguished, primal howl as he burst inside her. For that one split second, she reminded him of Melody again.

"Shit, Gil," she panted and she rolled off of him, "did I hurt you?"

"Nah," Gil gasped, "I'm okay."

And, physically, Gil was *quite* okay. But inside him something had torn, not a muscle or a ligament, but a wound that he thought time had finally healed. He forgot the pain temporarily, though, as Missy's lips brought him alive again. As long as parts of her were touching parts of him, he would probably be okay.

‡

"What movie are we going to see again?" Gil wonders, squinting as one of the multiplex cinema's spotlights flashes in his eyes.

"It's called *Shake It Up, Baby*."

"Oh, great!" Gil moans, as he hands over the cash for the movie tickets. "Any movie named after a 'fifties or 'sixties pop song is almost guaranteed to be paint-by-numbers pop crapola."

"I thought you *liked* songs from the 'sixties."

"I do. But I don't like the formulaic, feel-good-comedy-hit-of-the-summer bullshit the Hollywood studios keep grinding out these days."

"You don't like anything cute."

"I like *you*," Gil says, squeezing one of Missy's butt cheeks as she settles into the theatre seat beside him.

"Seriously, you don't like anything fun," she says.

"I like movies with *substance*, Missy."

"Oh, like that horrible thing you took me to see at that musty old dump last week? The one where the first, like, five hours had a bunch of apes running around, getting all excited about this big black box? What the hell was *that* shit?"

"That *shit*, as you call it, was *2001: A Space Odyssey*, one of the most brilliant conceptual movies ever filmed. The *black thing*, the Monolith, appears as a symbolic figure in the movie whenever humanity is about to take a step forward in evolution, and. . ."

"Boring!" Missy loudly yawns.

Gil is about to protest her interruption when she places her hand between his legs. Blood drains away from Gil's brain, and he drops the matter entirely. Without further complaint, Gil watches the cutesy actors on-screen traipse through the fill-in-the-blanks script of *Shake It Up, Baby*, sure that he will be more than adequately rewarded later in Missy's apartment.

‡

"Well, what do you want to do now?" Gil wonders, as they emerge from the theatre into the throbbing neon glare of the theatre's concourse.

She chirps, "Let's go dancing!"

"Uh. Do we have to?" Gil groans.

Gil shudders to think of the last time Missy dragged him out to one of those soulless dance clubs, just blocks from her apartment. Flashing lights, throbbing, melody-free music—more or less the late-night version of this stupid multiplex theatre, with the added bonus of clouds of choking cigarette smoke. There would be barely legal-age girls wearing glittering, skin-tight evening dresses and high heels, trying to contradict their look-at-me outfits by looking bored and uninterested. There would also be the requisite Cool Guys with flammable yet bullet-proof hair-dos, wearing open-collared black shirts and a-size-too-small dress pants, trying to appear more threatening than the next clone by folding their arms across their chests with their fists closed under their biceps to make them stick out more. If Gil felt awkward and out of place in the nightclub scene when he was Missy's age, he feels it even more now.

"Really, Missy," Gil reiterates, "I hate dance clubs."

"You hate everything I like!" Missy yelps.

"Well, not everything," Gil says, circling her waist with his arms and cupping her buttocks in his hands.

Missy wriggles out of his embrace. "Seriously, Gil. You hate everything I like. All you ever want to do is feel my ass, and take me back to my place to fuck me."

"Aw, c'mon, Missy," Gil manages, "you know that isn't true."

"Oh yeah?" she challenges, folding her arms and turning slightly away from him, "Tell me this, then, other than the sex, what do we do together that you actually enjoy?"

Gil looks stuck for a second, like somebody has pressed the "pause" button on the remote control for his body. Then he says, "I like to watch you dance. I really do. So let's just go to the dance club, okay?"

Gil is telling the truth. He hates the dance clubs themselves, but God, he loves to watch Missy dance, writhing and swaying and gyrating, just like she'll do later, beneath him, on top of him, standing with her back against the pastel-coloured wall of her bedroom, one leg wrapped around his back.

Missy says, "You only like to watch me dance because it gets you excited about fucking me."

Shit, Gil thinks. *Has she suddenly become psychic?*

"Aw, c'mon, Missy. What's got into you?" It's all he can think of to say.

She stands there with her hands on her hips, shaking her head. "The one thing that *isn't* getting into me tonight is you,

Gil," she says, her voice trembling. "I think it's time for us to part ways."

"What," Gil stammers, "what do you mean?"

"It's over, Gil. This isn't working."

"Can't we talk about this?"

"We don't talk about *anything*," she says. "Other than the fucking, we don't have anything in common."

"So it's over?" Gil says in a hush-hush voice, noticing that their conversation has drawn the attention of other nearby moviegoers. "Just like that?"

"Just like that, Gil," she says, with a cold tone Gil wouldn't have been able to imagine from her before now.

Missy starts to walk away, but then turns back to face him. "You know," she says, "I really liked you. I really thought you were different than the rest of them. But you're just another user, Gil, and I'm tired of being used."

Gil stands there in the foyer of the theatre, beneath the plastic *Starship Enterprise*. He does not bother to chase after Missy. He knows that everything she has said is essentially true.

Once upon a time, I was different than the rest of them, Gil thinks. *But I'm not that fucking sap any more.*

Gil feels relieved. No more yawning through lame-ass Hollywood movies, no more awkward twitching at the dance clubs. Yet, compacted into a tiny space deep inside himself, he also feels an impending sense of doom. Missy's bubbly, youthful nature, and her adventurous, generous sexuality had been like a ray of warm sunshine through a break in the clouds, but now Gil can feel those stormy clouds of anger and frustration and loneliness closing in on him. If he isn't careful, if he lets those clouds surround him, he'll wind up on his basement floor again, surrounded by empty booze bottles.

I'll be damned if I'm going to go through that shit again, Gil thinks. He straightens his back, sticks his chest out, and strides over to the escalator, which carries him down to street level. He pushes through the exit door, takes a deep breath of the thick, humid summer air, and strolls out into the dull orange glow of the streetlights.

‡

BLACK TAXI

A streetcar screeches past just as the DON'T WALK signal changes to WALK, and Gil sees his reflection, still dark-eyed and tired-looking, flicker like a movie from an old projector on the windows of a streetcar as it rushes past.

As he steps from the curb onto the street, he mutters to himself, "I *still* look like the living dead." Out of nowhere, a black taxi races toward the intersection, engine roaring, tires screeching. Gil is frozen in place, the taxi's headlights mesmerizing like squinting, glowing eyes, its grille locked in an aggressive sneer.

Gil's body snaps backward. He lands on his butt on the curb as the taxi screams through the red light. It takes him a second to realize that somebody's hands have grabbed him by the shoulders and pulled him out of the taxi's path at the very last second.

The black taxi screams away into the night, the roar of its engine swallowed by the thumping rhythms from the nearby nightclubs.

"So sorry about that, dude," says the shaggy-haired guy who crouches beside him. "Didn't mean to knock you down."

Gil looks at him with glassy eyes, dazed.

"Better than getting run over by a speeding taxi, though, eh, dude?" the guy says as he helps Gil to his feet.

The man who has just saved Gil's life could be anywhere from twenty to fifty years old. He's dressed in a Hawaiian-style print shirt, safari shorts, and a pair of hiking sandals. He has a shaggy mane of dirty blond hair, and his face is bristled with a three-day beard. He wears a pair of stylish sunglasses with lenses so black as to be opaque—a little strange, considering that the sun has already gone down. Pinned crookedly to the curled collar of his shirt is a single yellow rose, fresh and alive; the flower's welcome scent pushes through the smells of ozone, restaurant food, sewer gas, and exhaust fumes.

"Did anyone get the license number?" Gil wonders hazily.

"Of course not, man!" Gil's rumpled saviour chuckles. "Nobody ever sees anything!"

Through the guy's open collar, Gil notices gold monogram letters hanging from a gold chain: G R. *The same initials as mine,* Gil observes, but the thought is quickly swept away by the aftershock of the black taxi's near-miss.

"Thanks for grabbing me. I was nearly killed!"

"Haw haw haw," the guy chuckles. "They say your life flashes before your eyes when you're almost killed. Did your life flash before your eyes, man?"

"I don't think so," Gil says, "but I still think I owe you my life."

"Well, hey, dude," chuckles the disheveled hero, "I'm only in town for the night, and I've got nothing else going on, so why don't we go grab a beer. Unless you're meeting up with a chick or something—that takes priority, man!"

For a moment Gil sees an image of Missy's hot little body gyrating in the smoke-tinged strobe lights of a dance club, and wonders if he should go looking for her. *No,* he thinks, *forget it.*

"Nope, I'm free for the evening," Gil says.

"Well, then, Gilchrist," the stranger says, "since I'm from out of town, why don't you pick the place."

"How did you know my name?" Gil wonders.

"You told me just after I pulled you away from that taxi, didn't you?"

"I don't remember. I must have been pretty shaken up. I always call myself Gil, though, never Gilchrist."

The guy points to a restaurant just up the street from the multiplex theatre, and says, "How about that place?"

"Oh, sure," Gil says hazily. "It's a little touristy, but they have a well-stocked bar."

"Lead on, then, *Gil*," the stranger says.

‡

Gil and his rescuer are seated across from each other in a booth near the back of the restaurant. Gil glances around the large room, his brow furrowed.

Gil's rumpled guest asks, "Something wrong?"

"Things in here just look oddly familiar," Gil says.

"Didn't you say you've eaten here before?"

"Well, yeah, I come here all the time, but . . . it's hard to describe. There seem to be things in here I remember from *other* places."

Gil is used to the restaurant's dark wood walls, the black faux-marble floors, and the brushed stainless steel trim, but he didn't remember there being so many pastel-toned movie posters from the 'forties, Gil's favourite decade. There are other things, too, incongruous details he hadn't noticed until tonight. Set into a nearby wall is the grille from a 1968 Cougar, Gil's first car. On another wall, clashing with the rest of the décor, is a black-and-white snapshot of the rock band Rush in concert, the picture frame embossed with the words "Maple Leaf Gardens, June 1980"—coincidentally, not only Gil's first stadium rock concert, but his first experience with contraband liquor. A display case hangs next to their booth, with an assortment of unusual beer-bottle caps from around the world, exactly like the one that hung behind the bar at The Canadian National Tavern, a bar where Gil and his university buddies used to hang out and try to pick up girls—except for Gil, of course, who was still with Melody then, and who would never have dreamed of being unfaithful.

"Probably just déjà vu. Everybody gets that feeling sometimes."

"Yeah," says Gil, "I suppose. You know, I think you've forgotten to take off your sunglasses."

"No, I haven't forgotten," says the shaggy guy. "I've a bit of an eye problem. I have to keep them on."

"Sorry," Gil says, suddenly very embarrassed. "You know, you saved my life and I don't even know your name. What does the 'GR' around your neck stand for?"

"Oh, just call me 'GR.' I'd rather stay incognito for now."

"You someone famous?"

"Haw haw haw," chuckles GR, "not famous in a movie star sort of way. Nobody living here would know my face. My name, however, is rather well known."

"No problem, GR," Gil says, figuring that his guest is probably the playboy son of some reclusive old business tycoon, or some computer-geek-turned-millionaire-surfer-boy.

A waitress takes their drink orders. Gil orders a beer, and GR requests a Diablo, on the rocks. Gil's puzzled expression returns as the waitress saunters off towards the bar.

"What now?" GR wonders.

"That waitress. She looks just like one who worked at a diner where I used to go when I was seventeen. Has the same voice, too. Even walks like her. She used to secretly serve beers to my buddies and me."

"They say everyone has a double somewhere in the world," GR muses.

The waitress soon returns with their drinks.

GR asks, "Is your déjà vu gone now?"

Gil has just finished saying, "Yep, all back to normal now," when he notices someone even more familiar-looking than the waitress sitting in the booth across from them. The woman is at least ten years older than Gil, with her crow-black hair tied back, accentuating her sharp cheekbones, pointed nose, and thin, sculpted eyebrows. She is wearing glasses with thin rims and small lenses, of the type popular with academics and movie stars who want to look more intelligent than they are. This woman is the first type, a professor of psychology at the U of T.

"Holy crap," Gil gasps, "it's Acacia Dell!"

"Hmmm," says GR. He pauses to swish another sip of his cocktail around in his mouth, swallows slowly and deliberately. "Somebody you know?"

"Well, yes . . . *knew*, anyway."

"In the Biblical sense?" GR says slyly.

"Um, yeah, I suppose," Gil mumbles. "She used to be a girl-friend of mine."

"Ah—the one before Missy?" GR wonders.

"When did I mention Missy?"

"Didn't you tell me that she was your girlfriend, that you had just broken up with her this evening?"

"I don't remember telling you that, GR," Gil says uneasily.

"Haw haw haw," he chuckles, "if you didn't tell me, then how did I know?"

"Good point," Gil concedes.

"So she must be the older woman you were with *before* your six younger conquests, but just *after* Melody Lane, right?"

"I told you all that?" Gil says, shaking his head. "Man, did I hit my head when I fell? My memory is all screwed up."

This is turning into one weird evening, Gil thinks. He tentatively glances over at the woman sitting at the booth across from them. It is definitely Acacia Dell. After all this time, she hasn't changed a bit.

‡

PSYCH 223

During his second year in university, Gil Raphael was a student in Acacia Dell's Psychology 223 course. The official title of the course was The Psychology of Human Sexuality, a topic that consumed and tortured Gil. Professor Dell's theories on the subject were summarized in the opening statement of her first lecture of the semester: "Sex is not 'making love.' Sex is 'fucking.'"

This made most of the other students giggle and wriggle in their seats, but Gil disagreed bitterly with the professor's take on sex. His final, intense coupling with Melody had been more than just fucking, dammit! He spent hours in the social studies library digging up research, and when he submitted his bitter counterargument to Professor Dell's theory as his major term paper, she rewarded his work with a C- grade. Gil stomped angrily into her office, demanding an explanation.

In person, up close, inside her small, cluttered, incense-scented office, Acacia Dell looked softer than she did in the lecture hall. Her crisp black suit jacket with the padded shoulders and stiff lapels that made her look androgynous in the lecture hall now hung casually on the back of her chair, and Gil could see that she possessed actual breasts and hips.

"Hello, Mr. Raphael," she said. "You have some questions about the mark on your term paper?"

"The research supports my conclusions," Gil said stiffly.

"Well," the professor said, leafing through the pages of Gil's assignment, "as I've noted here, the studies you used are quite outdated. And you ignored a lot of stronger, more current evidence on the other side of things."

"Sex is not always just 'fucking,' as you put it," Gil said. "Sex can also be 'making love.'"

"Well, my own research attests to the contrary," she said. "The sexual act does not 'make' love, or anything else—it only releases tension, and makes you feel better."

Then Professor Dell leaned forward on her elbows, giving Gil a glimpse of cleavage. "However," she said, "I sense that you may have personal rather than academic reasons for wanting to disagree with these observations."

Gil shrugged, "What difference does it make?"

"Maybe you can convince me that yours is the circumstance that breaks the rules, in which case I would be happy to revise the grade on your paper."

So Gil told her all about Melody, about how he and Melody had played together as children, how he found her again in high school. They went to dances and movies and parties together. Finally, days before Gil was to go off to university in Toronto, he and Melody finally kissed, and, in that one moment, their friendship transformed into something else.

"Yes," said Professor Dell, "go on."

Gil went on.

‡

Shyly, tentatively, Melody's small fingers unbuttoned Gil's shirt, pushed it over his shoulders, and she slid his shorts down with a gentle sweeping motion. Her warm hands felt electric as they passed over his chest and legs, creating small spasms all through him. Scarcely able to breathe, Gil lifted her loose-fitting dress over her head. It was like unwrapping plain brown paper to discover a rare, glittering jewel wrapped up inside. Her body was a gift that he received slowly, savouring each square inch of flawless, milky flesh as it was revealed by the ascending fabric. They wrapped themselves around each other gently, slowly, as if the other was made of the thinnest skin of glass, as if this would all shatter if approached with too much force.

‡

"Hmmmm," said Professor Dell. "First time, right? I bet it was over quickly."

Gil shook his head. "No. It was as if time stopped," he said. "Which is why I feel so terrible now."

Acacia Dell leaned back in her chair, slowly exhaling, uncrossing then crossing her legs again. "You feel bad now because your body needs to have it again."

"I need to have *Melody* again," Gil said.

"No. You need to have *sex* again. You need to relieve the tension that's built up in you since then."

"There's more to it than that," Gil insisted.

She stood up from her desk, thrusting her chest forward. "Well, I'm famished," she said. "Would you like to continue our discussion over dinner?"

"Dinner?"

"You do eat, don't you?"

Gil's hostility toward the professor had dissipated during the few minutes in her office. He followed her to the faculty parking lot, where they climbed into her late model Volvo sedan.

"So, really, Mr. Raphael," she said, as she nudged the car into the early-evening traffic on University Avenue, "nothing you have told me so far contradicts my findings. You had sex, and now your body wants it again. You're confusing your physical need for sex with a need for this particular girl."

"I don't think so," Gil said, and continued with his story.

‡

Excited plans were made. Melody would take the train to Toronto to visit Gil as often as possible, and the following year, after Melody graduated from Faireville High, she would also attend the U of T, and she would move in with Gil. They talked on the phone every other night, sometimes into the early

morning. They would take turns describing to each other what
would be happening if they were together in Gil's single bed.

‡

"So far, you're still proving my theory more than disproving it,"
said the professor, as she locked the doors on the Volvo and led
Gil towards her favourite 'date' restaurant, an expensive little
haute cuisine restaurant tucked away in an alley in the Annex.
"You both became convinced of an emotional need for each other,
because you associated the relief of your self-pleasuring to each
other. That's essentially what phone sex is, you know."

"Let me tell you the rest of it," Gil said, as the *maitre d'* filled
their water glasses and lit the candles.

‡

When Melody finally arrived at Union Station for her first visit to
Toronto, neither she nor Gil could contain themselves. They
locked together in a swirling embrace, and not even the towering
buildings along Front Street could distract Melody from wildly
kissing Gil in the back seat of the green and orange taxi that car-
ried them to Gil's one-room basement apartment in Little Italy.
They didn't even make it to the bed the first time, as they tumbled
into each other at the bottom of the staircase, sweating, moaning,
gasping for breath, slowly and gently flowing into each other.

"Oh," she said, "I missed you so much."

"I missed you too," he said. "I needed to see you so badly."

‡

"You mean you missed the *sex*," Acacia Dell was quick to point out, the word *sex* sliding fluidly over her lips the same way she sipped the red wine from her glass. Gil had to admit that the professor had very attractive lips—they seemed less pursed, fuller than when she was lecturing her undergraduate class. "You needed to *fuck* her so badly," she whispered. The way she said *fuck* accelerated Gil's rising erection.

"I *still* miss her so much," Gil blurted out, probably a little too loudly for the restaurant's quiet ambiance.

"Until you find someone else to have sex with, that is," Acacia Dell said, looking at him over the top of her glasses. She motioned to the waiter for another bottle of wine, then she straightened in her chair and said, "But do go on. You've got my attention."

So, between delicious mouthfuls of braised duck, wood-grilled vegetables, risotto and Cabernet Sauvignon, Gil told Professor Dell the rest of the story. The professor wanted all the details, particularly the sexual parts. Gil didn't mind—it *was* her area of expertise, after all.

‡

After the first impassioned coupling of their reunion, Gil and Melody made love several more times, discovering new and more exciting ways of pleasuring each other. When they finally emerged from the basement apartment, it was early evening.

Gil took Melody to a place on Queen West popular with the student crowd. His tongue spiralled through a mouthful of Guinness as he watched her kiss the lip of a tall, slender margarita glass, her eyes aimed skyward like she'd seen this all before, as if this wasn't her first time in the big city. The ice in her glass crackled along with the chorus of screeching streetcar wheels, the plaintive echoed wailing of fire truck sirens six blocks away, the roar of subway trains rumbling up through sidewalk grates, haggling, shouting, a cacophony of languages, all of it a symphony meant for the two of them.

"Gil," she said. "We were meant to be here together in this city. It all feels just right."

‡

"It all surrounded me like rushing water," Gil told Acacia Dell. "It gave me a shivering feeling, like learning to swim."

Gil expected the professor to say something like "you mean 'the shivering feeling of learning to *fuck*,'" but instead she reached across that table, touched his hand, and said, "That's a beautiful way of describing it."

She ordered yet another bottle of wine, and, resuming her professional tone of voice, and said, "So. Tell me how it ended."

‡

For the next two months, Melody and Gil spoke on the phone nearly every night, each time talking each other up to a mutual sexual climax. Then Gil became busy with essay deadlines and midterm exams, and Melody worked equally hard at Faireville High, so she could get accepted to the U of T the next autumn, join Gil the next fall, and live happily ever after. The frequency of their phone calls decreased, but their intention to be together did not. Gil could hardly wait to see her again when he came home to Faireville for the Christmas holidays.

Then, one night in December, while Gil was studying for his European History exam, the phone rang. It was Melody.

"Gil," she said in a shaky voice, "we need to talk."

"What's wrong, sweetie?"

"God. There's no easy way to tell you this." A long pause. "I'm pregnant, Gil."

"But how?" Gil wondered, feeling his stomach tighten. "We used condoms every time!"

"Oh, Gil..." Another long pause. "I went out with the girls a while back. I got drunk. I met this guy..."

"Jesus, Melody," Gil said, biting his lip.

"I wanted to let him down easy. I was going to tell him about you, I just couldn't find the right moment."

There was silence on the phone line.

"Gil? Are you there?"

Gil was too shocked to speak. It was like watching his future fall over the edge of a cliff, and he was paralysed, powerless to do anything to stop it.

"I'm going to live with my parents until he can find a job," her voice quavered, "then we'll try to rent a cheap house outside of town. I'll get a job waitressing or something until the baby comes, then..."

"So this means you're not coming to Toronto, then?" Gil managed to say.

"Oh, Gil," Melody cried, "it all happened so fast. I'm so sorry. Please don't hate me."

‡

"See? See?" Acacia Dell chirped in her shrill lecturing voice. "I hate to have to be the one to point this out to you, but she *needed* the sex! She *liked* you, she maybe even *loved* you, but she *needed* the sex. So she found someone more conveniently located to provide it. It's the way human sexuality works."

"Then how come I still only want her?" Gil wondered.

"Look," the professor said, resuming her gentler voice, "you need to stop torturing yourself. You've been tricked, by culture and socialization, into believing that you need her, but all you need, physiologically and psychologically, is the sex." Her voice dropped to a whisper. "And I would be willing to prove that to you, if you're interested in, say, a little *experiment*."

The waiter stealthily placed the bill on the table. The price of the dinner was more than Gil's rent for the month, but he reached for it anyway. Acacia Dell snatched the bill from his hand, then looked him right in the eyes, and said, "On me."

Gil had only just finished fastening his seat belt when the professor stopped the Volvo by a curb on one of the residential streets in the Annex.

"You had better get out here," she said.

"Oh," said Gil, "Sure. I can take the subway home. Thanks for dinner."

"No, no," she laughed. "My garage isn't much wider than the car. If you don't get out now, you won't be able to get your door open after I'm parked."

"You mean you want me to come in?" Gil asked.

"Yes, Mr. Raphael," she said, smiling a tight-lipped smile. "I am inviting you to come in."

‡

Gil awoke the next morning wrapped in the off-white comforter of Acacia Dell's king-sized bed. He was lying on his side, the fingers of his right hand nestled in the professor's neatly trimmed patch of soft black pubic hair, his cheek pressed into the softness of her ample right breast.

The professor was so different from Melody. With Melody, it had been so tentative, so exploratory, but with Professor Dell it had been more like a competition, like combat, their bodies smashing together, sweat flying from their skins. Where Gil had taken a careful, gentle lead with Melody, Acacia pinned Gil to the white sheets, nailed him against the cream-coloured walls, barked out breathy orders: "Higher! Higher! Ohhhh, right there! Angle it up! Yes! Yessss! Finish me!" She guided his fingers to wherever she wanted them, pushed sensitive parts of herself to Gil's mouth, swayed and bent and arched to meet his thrusts, to absorb the most pleasure from his young body.

Gil slept more soundly that night than he had in months. When Professor Dell woke, she placed her hand over Gil's.

"You like?" she purred.

"Soft," Gil said.

"Shampoo, conditioner, and a gentle brushing every day," she said. "I trim it at least twice a week. It's good to keep the entrance to the sacred temple well manicured. I perfume it, too."

"I noticed," Gil said.

Gil rolled onto his back. If the professor kept her pubis well-prepared for sexual encounters, her bedroom was equally well appointed. There were gilt-framed mirrors, positioned for multi-angled views of events in progress on the bed. There were coral-coloured roses everywhere, incense sticks, candles, and small spotlights with dimmers, framed prints of Georgia O'Keefe's vaginal flowers and sleek phallic sculptures. There were tall brass bedposts for pushing off or hanging on.

"So," she asked. "Feeling better?"

Gil had to admit that he felt pretty good.

"Then our experiment was a success. You don't have to trick yourself into thinking that girl was what you wanted."

Melody. He'd been distracted, but now Gil thought about his last phone conversation with Melody.

‡

"Melody, please," Gil had begged, "I'll help you bring up your baby. Please! You can still be with me."

"Gil," Melody said evenly, "Jimmy has a right to be a father to his own child. I'm sorry, but this is reality. Maybe it would be easier on both of us if we agreed to stay out of contact for a while."

As much as it tore at Gil, he did as he was asked. He resisted the urge to call Melody again. Gil poured himself into his studies during the day, and at night he poured liquor into himself until he passed out.

‡

"Well," Acacia Dell said, springing out from under the sheets, wrapping herself quickly in a white terrycloth robe, "we both have a class to be at in a couple of hours. You had better get going."

She wandered into the *en suite* bathroom.

"I think I'll raise the mark on your term paper to an A," her voice echoed from the bathroom tiles, "but of course you'll have to promise me that last night must remain between the two of us."

"Sure, no problem," Gil said, sliding out from under the covers and standing beside the bed. "Could we maybe get together again sometime? Do you like 1940s movies?"

Acacia Dell reappeared in the bathroom doorway, her well-maintained pubis and one silver-dollar-sized nipple peeking through the opening in her bathrobe. Gil's penis lifted up in the air.

"Why don't you just shower here with me," Professor Dell said, shrugging her robe onto the floor.

‡

From that point on, Gil and the professor met once or twice a week, sometimes for dinner, sometimes to view an art exhibit, sometimes to catch an old movie at the local repertory theatre, but always concluded by an aggressive romp in her bedroom. In class, Gil was careful to address her as Professor Dell, but in the evenings he called her Acacia.

One night, as they rested atop the white comforter between bouts, Gil told her he thought he might be falling in love with her.

"For crying out loud, Gil," she scolded, "haven't you learned anything?" She straddled him, and said, "Saying that you're *falling in love* is just a cutesy, socialized way of telling someone you want more of *this!*"

And she absorbed him once again.

‡

No matter how Acacia felt about it, though, Gil believed he was falling in love with her. Normally, their meetings were carefully orchestrated to ensure minimum exposure to other students and professors, but one evening Gil was feeling impulsive, and he decided to just drop in at Acacia's house. He brought along a bottle of good champagne, a bouquet of the coral-coloured roses she favoured, and a small bottle of the expensive perfume she liked to spray between her legs. Without enough cash left for the subway, Gil walked all the way to her house.

He knocked on the door. No answer. He walked around the tuft of shrubbery by the front door of the house, and peered through the little window on the door of the attached garage. Acacia's Volvo was parked inside. *She must be home*, Gil thought.

Just then, he heard the front door open, and the sound of Acacia's laughing voice. And another voice as well.

"Thanks, Professor!" the voice said. "Another tutorial session next week, then?"

"You can call me Acacia when we're off campus," she said.

Both voices giggled.

Gil watched from behind the shrub as the professor's male guest swaggered away. Gil recognized him as the psychology grad student who sometimes helped the professor run her undergraduate lab sessions. Enjoying a session of his own, apparently.

Just as Acacia turned to close the door behind her, Gil jumped out into the open.

"Gil!" she yelped, startled.

"Hello, Acacia."

"What are you doing here, Gil? We didn't set anything up, did we?"

"I brought you some flowers."

"Oh, that's awfully nice of you, Gil, but I don't think I can have you in right now."

"Who was *that*?" Gil demanded.

"Oh, Gil," she said, taking a step through the door, "you should have known that this was not exclusive."

Gil tossed the bouquet on the sidewalk. The vase shattered. Professor Dell took a step back inside.

Through a crack in the door, she said, "Stop fooling yourself like this, Gil! Haven't you learned anything?"

Gil pulled out the bottle of perfume. "I brought you some of the scent you like to spray on the garden of your sacred temple," he said.

He raised the small bottle high above his head, then hurled it to the concrete. The bottle smashed, and the thick, floral scent diffused through the air.

"Now everyone who passes by can smell it," Gill rumbled, and stomped away into the night.

Gil wandered all the way to High Park, where he sat on the grass and guzzled down the bottle of champagne, fitting right in with other nocturnal occupants who lazed around in the shadows. The alcohol burned his empty stomach and thundered through his bloodstream. He looked up at the stars, which spun in a blur above him, and resolved that he would never again fool himself about love.

"If somethin' seems too good to be true," he shouted at the night, "it prob'ly is. You win, Professor! There is no love. There is no hope. All that stuff is just illusions!"

‡

BLACK TAXI (REVISITED)

This is what the bystanders see just after Gil leaves the multiplex theatre after being dumped by Missy, as he steps from the curb onto the street:

Out of nowhere, a black taxi races toward the intersection, engine roaring, tires screeching. Gil is frozen in place, the taxi's headlights mesmerizing like squinting, glowing eyes, its grille locked in an aggressive sneer. The grille snaps, shatters into plastic shards as it bites into Gil's legs, the hood buckling with a loud smack from the impact of his torso slamming against the hood. Gil's body careens over the car, an elbow and knee leaving spiderweb cracks in the windshield glass, his pelvis denting the roof. The taxi's trunk lid pops open as Gil bounces from it and rolls in the street.

His body comes to rest face down, his arms and legs splayed awkwardly on the blacktop. The black taxi screams away into the night, the roar of its engine swallowed by the thumping rhythms from the nearby nightclubs. Nobody thinks to make note of the cab's license number. People begin to run towards Gil's body.

Someone cries out, "Call an ambulance!"

Another crouches down, grips Gil's flaccid wrist, shouts out, "My God, he's dead!"

This is what the bystanders see.

What Gil himself sees is something quite different. He has been pulled from harm's way at the last moment by a shaggy bystander wearing a Hawaiian shirt, sandals, and sunglasses with deep black lenses, a bystander whose name has the same initials as his own, a man with whom he has shared many drinks, dinner, dessert, and coffee, with whom he is now arguing for the right to pay the bill.

"Please," Gil says, "it's the least I can do. You saved my life, after all."

"I'm afraid that is not the case, poor soul," GR says.

"Geeze, I must be hammered," Gil laughs. "Did your voice just get deeper?"

GR unexpectedly grips Gil's wrist tightly in his bony fingers, and a chill races through Gil's entire body. With his free hand, GR removes the sunglasses from his face to reveal empty black eye sockets. The fresh yellow rose on his collar shrivels, turns crisp, dry, and black.

Gil says, "Holy shit!"

"You're half right, as usual, Gilchrist," GR says.

Gil cannot free his wrist from the bony grip. He glances around the room in panic, trying to catch someone's eye. It seems that everyone he has ever known now occupies a seat at the restaurant: Missy is seated at a large table, chatting casually with five other young women about her age, all of whom recently dated Gil for periods of time ranging from two to six weeks. At an adjacent table, Professor Acacia Dell sits with the young man Gil caught her with that night he dropped in at her house. At a large table close to the entrance to the restaurant sit Gil's parents and his extended family, laughing among themselves. At other tables throughout the room are all his former and current friends, teachers, professors, colleagues, superiors, subordinates . . . everybody he has ever known, from the kid who made him eat a worm in kindergarten, to his high school buddies Dave, Jeff, Jamie, and Chris, to the guy who sold him his first car, to the girl who let him feel her budding breasts under her Camp Kitcheekadoodle T-shirt. . . *everybody* is somehow here at this restaurant right at this very moment. Yet nobody sees him.

"Your life is flashing before you," GR says evenly. "You must come with me now."

Gil tries to resist, but his body floats along behind as he is tugged behind his dinner companion toward the kitchen at the back of the restaurant.

"Help me!" Gil cries out to a waitress—the one who used to secretly serve beers to Gil and his buddies at the local diner when they were only seventeen. She acts as if he isn't there. "I'm being kidnapped!" He screams to the oblivious chefs, who continue slicing and stirring and cooking in the kitchen, just like they used to do in the cafeteria in Gil's residence in university.

"Oh, I almost forgot my little spiel," GR says in a bored tone of voice, like an old cop reciting an arrested man's rights: "I am the Grim Reaper, I am Death, the time has come to reap what has been sown, yadda yadda yadda. . ."

"You can't be the Grim Reaper!" Gil cries. "The Grim Reaper doesn't dress like a surfer dude!"

"Haw haw haw," the Reaper chuckles, "you want the sickle and the black cloak and all that?"

"I want to keep living!" Gil begs. "I want to live!"

"That's not what you told me in there," the Grim Reaper scolds. "You have no reason left to live. You have given up hope. You told me so yourself."

"I never said that!"

"You didn't tell me with your *mouth*, but with your head. I can read your thoughts, and your memories too."

"I haven't given up hope!"

"From your own recent memory I quote: *There is no love. There is no hope. All that stuff is just illusions.*"

"I didn't mean it like *that*! I'm not ready to *die*!"

"But you've been living like a walking dead man for some time now, Gilchrist."

With his free hand, the Reaper pushes open the exit door at the back of the restaurant's kitchen. Gil is paralyzed, unable to speak or breathe or move when he sees what is beyond the door, for it is something his brain cannot quite comprehend. What he sees is *nothing*. Not darkness, not empty space, just *nothing*. Darker than darkness, emptier than emptiness. The complete lack of existence. *Nothing*.

Gil wriggles, kicks, contorts himself, but cannot break free. He cranes his neck to look back at the assembled crowd in the restaurant.

"Help me! Someone help!" he screams.

Frantically, his eyes scan the room for someone who can hear or see him.

"Melody! Where's Melody? Melody, help me, save me!"

Gil can't see her anywhere.

"Where is she?" Gil begs the Reaper. "Where's Melody?"

"How should I know?" the Grim Reaper says, aiming his empty eye-holes at Gil. "It's *your* life flashing before *your* eyes, Gilchrist. I'm just here to take you away."

The Reaper turns, resumes towing the weightless Gil towards the back of the restaurant.

"No no no no no!" Gil hollers. "God help me! God help me!"

The Grim Reaper sighs, and his grip on Gil's wrist loosens slightly, but not enough for Gil to struggle free.

"He's got a soft spot for you, Gilchrist Raphael," the Reaper shrugs. "Thank your parents for giving you such a providential name."

Gil feels momentarily calm, entranced. He looks around the restaurant again, then into the Reaper's shadowy eye sockets, and he says two words: "Where's Melody?"

"Hmm," the Grim Reaper says, "Would you like to try to find her? Well, then." The Reaper spreads his fingers open, releasing Gilchrist Raphael from his grip. "Consider this a second chance."

Gil turns and runs, away from the Reaper, away from the door full of *nothing*, back towards existence, towards a second chance, towards *something*.

"Haw haw haw," the Grim Reaper laughs, "we must do this again sometime. *Dude*."

Then, the Reaper slides into nothing, out of existence, closing the door behind him.

☦

On the street outside the restaurant, sprawled on the pavement like a broken marionette, Gil Raphael draws a breath.

"Wait! Wait! He's breathing!" calls out the bystander who has crouched beside him to check his pulse. "He's alive!"

When the paramedics arrive, they will strap Gil to a stretcher and load him into the back of an ambulance. The doctor in the emergency room at St. Michael's will set a few broken bones, swab the abrasions, and stitch up the cuts. Gil will be kept for observation, then released the next day with a pair of crutches and a prescription for painkillers. Nobody at the hospital will suspect that Gil's survival is a miracle.

Gil will tell the doctor that he smells wild lilacs, like the ones that grew in his hometown when he was a kid. The doctor will sniff at the dry, antiseptic air of the hospital, say "Hmm," and he will schedule a return visit for Gil to have a brain scan.

A nurse will help Gil to a pay telephone, where she will inform him that he can "call a cab, or whatever." He will not be aware that, on the exterior wall of the hospital, directly above where he will be standing, is a huge image of St. Michael, the hospital's namesake, his angel wings spread open. Nor will he be aware of the dead body being wheeled past, just behind him, a white sheet pulled over its face.

The body will have been found inside a now-aging Volvo sedan, parked inside one of the few attached garages in the Annex, only inches wider than the actual car itself. The windows on the car will have been rolled down, the inside of the garage sealed airtight with duct tape, the Volvo's engine left running to fill the tight space with noxious carbon monoxide fumes. The body will still have a crumpled suicide note clenched in its left hand, which will read, *"I'm just so tired of being lonely."*

Unaware of the body being rolled past him, or of the angel hanging above him just outside, Gil will lean on his crutches, and, with his uninjured right hand pointer finger, he will punch a series of numbers on the keypad of the payphone, aware of only one thing.

HOPE

It is a sunny, hot, crackling-dry day in the farm country just outside a little southwestern Ontario town called Faireville. A young mother peers through the screen window above the kitchen sink inside the little bungalow she rents from the farmer up the lane. The breeze softly ruffles the once-white curtains, and she pushes her face against the whisper of air, straining to absorb even the slightest relief from the heat, inhaling the scent from the wild lilac bushes that grow everywhere around here.

She calls out to her two small girls, who are giggling outside, running through the sprinkler on the otherwise parched lawn.

"Laura! Rachel! Lunch time, girls!"

Both of her daughters have the same honey-coloured hair and deep blue eyes as their mother. Rachel, who is nearly four now, wasn't born yet when her father ran off. Nine-year-old Laura rarely mentions him anymore. Their mother has tried very hard to forget him, too, to forget what she gave up for him, to let the resentment and anger evaporate from her body. *Better off just the three of us,* she thinks.

She stirs the small pot full of Alphagettios that simmer on the stovetop. She hates serving them meals from a can, but the girls love this stuff. The noodles are shaped like letters, and Laura likes playing a game with her little sister to teach her the alphabet as they eat. When the girls come in, she will pour them grape juice, butter some Wonderbread, give them one small chocolate-chip cookie each when their bowls are clean.

They're good girls, she thinks. *I really can't complain.*

A welcome gust of wind whistles through the window screen, flipping over a page of the thin local newspaper, *The Faireville Gleaner.* An ad on the newly turned page tells her that *Casablanca* is playing at the recently restored Faireville Palace theatre, and she smiles. Someone she knew once used to love old movies and old movie theatres; he would have taken her to see it for sure.

The phone rings. Probably one of those damned telemarketers. She stirs the bubbling Alphagettios with the wooden spoon in her right hand while stretching her left arm towards the phone. Her outstretched fingertips nab the receiver on the third ring.

"Yep?" she says, stretching the spiral cord of the receiver over to the stove.

There is silence on the line.

"Hello? Hell-o-ooooh?" she sings. "Anyone there?"

"Melody?" the voice on the other end of the line finally says.

"Gil?" she says.

"Hi, Melody."

The wooden spoon hits the floor, spattering orange tomato sauce and a T-shaped noodle on the faux-brick vinyl floor.

"Gil? Gil Raphael? Is that really you?"

"Yeah," Gil replies, "it's really me."

Acknowledgements

"Sky and Earth" appeared in the *New Orphic Review,* Spring, 2000, and won first place in the *New Orphic* Short Story Contest.

"The Doppler Effect" was published in *The Nashwaak Review,* Fall, 2002.

"Sky and Earth" and "The Doppler Effect" were also finalists in the fiction category of The New Century Writer Awards, 2002.

"The Jazz Man's Girl" and "The Twilight Girl" appeared in the Spring 2003 issue of the *New Orphic Review.* "The Twilight Girl" also won the 2002 Lawrence House Centre for the Arts Short Story Competition.

"Destiny's Telescope" was originally published as a prose poem in Cranberry Tree Press's *2001: A Space Anthology,* 2001.

"Sandcastles, Waves" was published in the anthology *Love*

and Longing in the Near North, Catchfire Press, 2000. It also received an Honourable Mention in the 1996 *Paragraph* Short Fiction Contest.

"Lost and Found" was chosen by guest editor Camilla Gibb to appear in the Fall 2004 issue of *Descant.*

"Traffic Jam" appeared in *Winners Circle Anthology* 10, by The Canadian Authors' Association, 2002, and won an Honourable Mention in their short story competition.

"Symbols" was featured in *The Breath* E-Zine in September 2003.

"Reasons" originally appeared as a poem in the author's poetry chapbook, *Guessing at Madeline* (Cranberry Tree Press, 1998), which won the 1997 Cranberry Tree Press Poetry Chapbook Competition.

"Adventure Therapy" (from "Black Taxi") appeared in slightly different form in the Spring 2005 issue of *Storyteller* as "Rebound." Also, a little piece of "Black Taxi" appeared as "Post Script" in the Spring 2005 issue of *Rampike.* Another little snippet from "Psych 223" ("Black Taxi" again) won third prize in the West End Writers Club 2004 writing contest. The piece was called "That Scent."

Also...

A few (but not all) of the quotations made by the character Doctor Hans Vetter in the story "Traffic Jam" were originally quoted in the great travelogue *The Songlines,* by Bruce Chatwin.

A note about "Black Taxi": According to Western tradition, Yellow Roses mean friendship and the promise of a new beginning. Orange Roses show desire and enthusiasm. Coral Roses convey desire. Black Roses signify Death.

"The Jazz Man's Girl" is composed entirely of single-syllable words. It is also (perhaps not coincidentally) the shortest story in this book.

Gratitude

I would like to thank editor Wayne Tefs for his wise and subtle guidance during the completion of this book. Everyone should read Wayne's books. Go get them! Go get them all! Go now!

Thanks also to Todd Besant, Sharon Caseburg, and the rest of the crew at Turnstone Press for their skill and professionalism in producing this book. Everyone should read Turnstone books. Go get them! Go get them all! Go now!

I would also like to express my thanks to all the editors at all of the magazines and journals that published early versions of some of the stories in this collection (please see the acknowledgements page). Everyone should read all of these magazines—you know what to do.